CAVE WRITINGS 2013

CAVE WRITINGS 2013

A PATO'S CAVE ANTHOLOGY

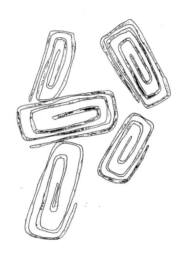

PATO'S CAVE PRESS

PORT TOWNSEND, WASHINGTON

MMXIII

Pato's Cave Press

938 Water Street, #301

Port Townsend, Washington 98368

Text and Illustration Copyright © Ezra Aguilar, Ella Ashford,

Rowan Halpin, Sam Heron, Odette Jennings, River R. Kisler,

Lemonie, E. M. Penrose, Korbyn Reimnitz, Ruevear, Isaac

Steimle, Anna Tallarico, Story Walsh, O. J. R. Weinblatt Dey,

and Ella Wiegers, 2013.

ISBN: 978-1-304-28183-8

Jacket illustrations by Ruevear.

Printed in the United States of America.

The Cave writers dedicate this book
to their dedicated parents.

Pato's Cave is the writing studio of children's author Patrick Jennings. It was founded in 2009, and is located in Port Townsend, Washington. Each week, young writers visit to create and discuss literature. This is the Cave's first anthology.

It's funny how much easier it is to write

when you're excited about it.

~River Kisler, June 11, 2013

CAVE WRITINGS 2013

CONTENTS

ROWAN HALPIN

Martha

Martha ran a hand over her sweating forehead and looked up Riddle Hill. She was almost at the top. For twenty minutes or more she had climbed, which was quite an achievement. It took grown men much longer to get as far as she had in such a short time.

Martha was angry with her mother, who had scolded her for spilling a bucket of milk. But really, it wasn't Martha's fault. The cows here were big, strong animals, and when they were spooked, they tended to stomp anything underfoot: buckets, mud, and even little girls' hands. That was the reason her mother had sent her to town, to fetch milk. A big family such as theirs needed a lot. She had hidden the two glass milk jugs at the bottom of the hill, not wanting to lug them, and set off up the hill. Her mother would not expect her home until much later. Their farm was the farthest from town. Four miles each way. Normally it would take her all day, but she had hitched a ride on a passing hay wagon.

As she reached the top of the hill, the first of the gravestones came into view. They were old stones, crumbling and weather-worn. Old oak trees grew all around, their gnarled branches reaching towards the sky. It was a short walk to Malcolm's grave and took Martha no time at all. She sat with her back to the headstone and looked out over the bluff.

Malcolm had been young when he died, only nine. Martha had been twelve at the time. Even after two years, she heard his screams in her sleep. No one knew what killed Malcolm. He yelled one night and woke everyone in the house, but when they reached his room, he was dead, his face stiffened in a scream.

• • •

Martha jerked awake. Her teacher's hand was gripping her shoulder.

"Oh, ma'am, I'm sorry," Martha began, but she

was silenced by her teacher's warm smile.

"It is quite all right, dear. I was just telling the class about our local Scottish lore."

Martha sat up and watched as the teacher strode back to the front of the room. She had been dreaming about Malcolm.

"Anyway, back up here, class, thank you. Yes, here we are. There are two graveyards in the area, the one atop Riddle Hill and the one that is in town. However the one atop Riddle Hill is rumored to be special…"

• • •

Riddle Hill was much harder to climb in the dark. Not to mention the fact that Martha was hampered by the large, thatched sack and shovel she was carrying. When she reached the top, she lit the small lantern she had brought. Navigating the gravestones at night was very difficult, but with her lantern it was easier. Finally, she found his grave. Setting aside the sack and placing the lamp on the ground, she began to dig. The ground wasn't hard, but neither was it soft. After an hour she had dug a good-sized hole in the ground. Her shovel made contact with something wooden. It was Malcolm's coffin. She dug more, and soon it was totally visible. With much effort, she heaved the heavy box up and out of the hole. She stared down at the aged coffin, horrified at what she would find inside. She took a deep breath and pried open the lid.

"Malcolm, Malcolm, Malcolm," she chanted.

• • •

Martha swabbed her brow with her sleeve as she patted down the last mound of dirt. She threw her shovel aside and looked at the filled hole. Her teacher had said that if the smallest amount of air could penetrate the grave, it wouldn't work. She turned and looked at the sack on the ground. It wasn't big enough. Ivan Shott's feet stuck out. She bent over and grabbed the bottom of the sack. She heaved Ivan's body over to Malcolm's now unoccupied grave, and struggled to lower him in. That done, she began filling the hole in with dirt. She then sat down beside the headstone that read IVAN SHOTT. Malcolm would be with her again soon.

The switching of two people's bodies was an old ritual that yielded incredible results. If you said the name of the person you wanted returned while digging him up, then placed his body in another person's grave, he would awaken. When Malcolm awoke, he would have Ivan's memories, personality, and intention.

Martha was scared of what she had done, but felt it was for the best. Malcolm would come home and everything would return to normal. Martha shivered. Leaving Malcolm's grave, she grabbed up the bag and shovel then sprinted back down the hill.

•   •   •

Little did Martha know, Ivan was not stable. Not

stable at all. Ivan Shott had been criminally insane. He had murdered his whole family, then, over a period of time, consumed them. Ivan killed himself afterwards. No one ever discovered what he had done, and no one ever would. They buried Ivan and were done with it. But Ivan's insanity would live on. Malcolm would continue it for him.

ANNA TALLARICO

Excerpt from Thunderheart

"It wasn't your fault," said Destiny to Becky at lunch.

"Thanks, Dessie," said Becky, taking a sip of juice.

"Wow." Stacy and her friends, Erin and Kelsey, appeared next to their table, smirking. "Passing notes? Everybody else stopped doing that in, like, third grade."

Destiny stood. "Shut up!" she snapped, glaring at Stacy.

"So Becky's going to get help in math," Stacy continued, ignoring Destiny. "So, does that mean she's, like, special needs?"

"What's wrong with that?" Becky mumbled, but Destiny saw her reddening.

"Stacy, I'm telling Ms. Blake if you keep

7

going," Destiny said, clenching her teeth.

"You're going to tell on me? Tattletale..." Stacy laughed. "Passing notes and sucking up to the teacher. What a dork." Her friends laughed, too.

Destiny felt herself redden with anger. And then, like magic, something appeared in her hand. She glanced down and almost screamed. She was gripping a glowing sword with a silver hilt and blue blade. The blade pulsed light as she squeezed it. Was this some sort of toy sword that someone put in her hand as a joke? She carefully touched it and saw blood. It was real.

"Oh, my, g—get out of here!" Stacy shrieked, pushing Kelsey and Erin out of the way in her haste to get away from Destiny. They ran, stumbling over each other, to the other end of the cafeteria. Strangely, no one seemed to notice them, or Destiny's sword, and when Destiny looked at them again, Stacy and her friends were talking and laughing at their table like nothing had happened.

Becky stared at her lunch tray. "There's nothing

wrong with having trouble with math," she told herself quietly, but she didn't look like she believed it.

"Becky, what just happened?" Destiny exclaimed. "What's going on? What is this—" She raised her hand, but the sword had disappeared. "Where'd it go?" she whispered, ducking under the table to search the floor. It wasn't there.

"Destiny, there's nothing wrong with needing extra help in math, right?" Becky asked nervously. "Stacy is going to torment me forever, but…"

"Yeah, about Stacy. What just happened?"

"What do you mean? You just told her to go away and she did. What's the big deal?"

"I didn't tell her to go away! A glowing blue sword, like, appeared in my hand, and I scared her away and she ran—" Destiny realized she was making no sense. Becky stared at her. "I mean, I guess I *could've* imagined it…"

"Um, yeah…" Becky scooted away from Destiny and picked up her tray. "I'm done," she muttered, standing up. "See you back in class." She walked quickly away, leaving Destiny alone.

What *had* happened? She gazed around the cafeteria. Everything looked normal. Then, out of the corner of her eye, she spotted an old woman looking at her. Destiny started, but when she looked more closely, she was gone.

• • •

Destiny glanced nervously at Becky as they walked down the hall towards the principal's office. She remembered the creepy old woman, and the even creepier sword. Becky had avoided her the rest of the day, and it was kind of awkward to be walking side by side without talking.

They paused before entering. Becky looked at Destiny and crossed her fingers. Destiny sighed and slowly pushed the door open.

It was very cold inside. The window was open, even though it was November. There were countless awards on the walls, along with pictures of the school every year since 1976, outlined in pressed leaves. The desk was littered with models of endangered animals, nature brochures, and green folders. Destiny wondered how much real work she actually did.

The principal, whose real name was Ms. Clark but wanted to be known as Ms. Green, sat in a black chair, reading a book on world peace. She wore her thick, frizzy salt-and-pepper hair down so that it puffed up weirdly in the back, a black shirt with a big picture of Earth on the front, and an ankle-long black and green skirt. She raised her head as she heard Destiny and Becky walk in.

"Hi!" she said brightly, indicating two plastic toddlers' outdoor chairs that sat in front of her desk.

Destiny and Becky, uncomfortable, sat down, wincing at the loud creaking noise the plastic made. The chairs felt like they would break any moment.

"Have you two been making trouble again?" The principal beamed at them with a too-happy face.

Destiny raised her eyebrows. Again? This was

the first time she had been in here since fourth grade, and technically that hadn't been her fault.

"Passing notes is a waste of precious paper," continued the principal, shaking her head, her many bracelets, necklaces, and earrings jangling. "The poor forests will thank you kindly if you don't do that anymore!"

Destiny and Becky glanced at each other.

"Changing your heart will help the environment!" Ms. Green laughed, then escorted them out of the office. "Remember! Be good to the environment! Make better choices!" And she shut the door softly.

Destiny heaved a sigh and sagged against the wall. "Wow."

"Wow," Becky echoed. She started down the hall and stopped. "Are you coming? Mom's probably waiting for us."

Destiny blinked and followed Becky. She had been wondering if she should tell Ms. Green about what happened at lunch. She would just have to tell her parents. *That* would be interesting.

EZRA AGUILAR

Gandul's Revenge

Illustrated by O. J. R. Weinblatt Dey

As Gandul chopped an orc in half, he remembered
what an army of orcs had done to his farm. Another
one ran at him. Gandul blasted a blue ball of energy,
instantly blowing up two orcs, reminding him of how
orcs had blown up both his cows. More orcs were
jumping out of their ships. The dwarves' catapult shot
a flaming rock and sunk one of the ships. The other
ship had been docked for a long time. A dwarf shot a
crossbow at the orcs' leader. When they saw their
leader fall with an arrow in his side, they ran towards
their ship, but didn't get very far before Gandul and
his dwarves were upon them. Gandul and his army
hacked and hewed at the orcs until there was nothing
left but broken limbs and unrecognizable shapes.

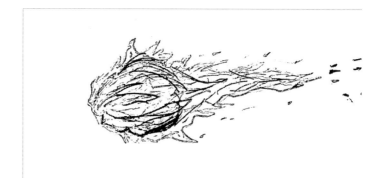

Even though Gandul's army had beaten the orc army, however, the Evil Lord still had to be annihilated.

• • •

Gandul was sharpening his ax among the bloody aftermath of the battle, when his advisor walked into the room and said, "The orc army is grouping for another attack."

"Okay. Make sure this time we destroy their flame hurler," Gandul said, "I'm going to go check on the infirmary. You can ready the troops."

The orc army had split up into smaller groups. They encircled the dwarf encampment. But the dwarves had placed many sharp pieces of wood around their fort so that when the orcs attacked they would be stopped or killed.

When the orc army attacked, the dwarves were ready. An ugly green orc ran at a dwarf and stabbed him in the hand with his spear, leaving the dwarf pinned to the ground. The dwarf swung his heavy war mallet and crushed the orc's skull. A different orc stabbed the dwarf in the back.

Gandul rushed over to the flame hurler, chopped it in half with his ax, then yelled, "Retreat! Retreat! Back to the fort!"

The dwarves all turned and ran from the battleground to their fort. At the fort, Gandul removed his armor.

• • •

The next morning Gandul woke up to find he was sore from the tips of his hair to the ends of his toes. He was washing his hands when his commander burst into his room.

"The orc army is coming for another attack!" the commander said.

Gandul threw on his chain mail and his thickest armor.

He ran to the battlements and yelled to a guard "Get me a crossbow!"

By the time the guard came back with the crossbow, the orc army had gotten a lot closer. When the orc army finally was in shooting range, it was night. The ground so far below was as black as a raven's wing. Gandul and his guards couldn't see a thing. Suddenly, a torch zoomed out of the gloom, and bounced off the iron gate; Gandul shot his crossbow. He heard a groan. He shot again and heard another groan.

"Get baskets full of rocks and dump them over the side of the parapet!"

The guards ran to obey. Gandul lit a torch and threw it to the ground over the side of the wall. It hit an orc and burst into flames. The orc screamed and started running around. The flames revealed where all the other orcs were hiding. When the guards got back, Gandul had memorized where the orcs were hiding. He told the guards where to dump the baskets of rocks.

"On the count of three! One…two…three!" They dumped the rocks over the side. The screams were drowned out by the sound of smashing bones. The dwarves climbed off the wall and were shocked by the number of orcs that lay dead on the ground.

After the battle, Gandul realized that if he could win the next battle he could end the war between the dwarves and the orcs, so he decided to take five hundred men and sail all the way to the Evil Lord's castle and lay it under heavy siege.

• • •

One day when Gandul was chopping firewood, he heard a twig snap behind him, then felt a canvas bag being pulled over his head. He felt his arms being yanked up behind his back and someone began to tie them together. Gandul struck out with his leg and heard a grunt of pain. Whoever had ambushed him hadn't been able to tie his arms completely, so Gandul wriggled his right wrist free and pulled the bag off his head. When his eyes adjusted to the light, he was staring into the green-blue face of the orcs' king, Zalahov. Zalahov's right eye had been gouged out by Gandul's ax in the past.

Gandul knocked Zalahov over the head with the butt of his ax, stunning the orc. Gandul ran towards his camp. "Get into the boats!" he yelled. "The orcs found us!"

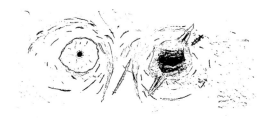

The dwarves got into their longboats and pushed away from the shore. Gandul barely had enough time to jump onto the back of the last boat to leave the harbor.

• • •

After he had been at the castle for a week, he was in a tent giving a speech when a flaming rock smashed into the side of the canvas wall. Gandul jumped to his feet and ran to get the army ready. When it was, Gandul told them his plan.

"I will climb through the window of the castle. You will wait outside and defend our people."

The army rushed into battle. Then Gandul ran to the edge of the castle. An orc threw his ax at him, slicing another orc's head off. Gandul started running again; he dodged an arrow and jumped over a pile of bodies not knowing how many had been dwarves. He ran straight into a dwarf the size of small child with hair the color of soil and eyes tilted downward in a grimace. His arms hung loosely from his shoulders

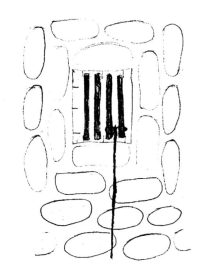

like a loose door hinge. Gandul knew that it couldn't

be anyone other than his cousin, Altor.

"Hello, Altor. Would you like to come with me to infiltrate the castle?"Altor turned his head. "Yes, Gandul, I'll come."

Gandul threw a grappling hook up the side of the castle. It latched to a barred window. "After you, Altor," Gandul said.

Altor started to climb up the rope. Gandul followed him. When Gandul got to the second floor he saw Altor lying on the floor with an arrow in his left arm, a pool of blood surrounding him. Suddenly an arrow flew at Gandul, but missed him by centimeters. Then five orcs ran through the door. One threw a spiky ball. Gandul dodged it. When it landed, it blew up, throwing Gandul out the window. He landed on an orc's stomach with a *squelch*.

Gandul swung his ax. It glowed blue and chopped many orcs in half. Blood spurted everywhere, but Gandul continued to fight. The orc army finally decided to retreat back to their castle. The dwarf army (which was now only fifteen dwarves) where forced to leave. They hid in ditches and holes and even haystacks. Gandul had started stealing food to eat.

"I do not want to steal but I do not want to starve," Gandul said to his army.

• • •

One night Gandul was sneaking around of the castle when he heard three orcs talking about the Evil Lord's plans. He knelt down behind them to listen.

The biggest and bulkiest of the three said, "The Evil Lord is planning to hire some new servants."

The second orc said, "I heard that he was going to hire new soldiers!"

The third one left to get some more firewood, while the other two continued to argue. Gandul snuck away, satisfied, back to the dwarves' camp.

In the morning he woke to the sound of a crow. He knew what he must do to get revenge on the Evil Lord for what he had done to his farm. That morning he put a straw hat on his head, put on some ragged clothes, then he bought a pitchfork for two silver pieces, and, he was a farmer! Leaving his army behind he set out onto the winding road.

After an hour of steady walking Gandul arrived at the castle. It looked warm and comfortable from the outside; the grass was green and the flowers were blooming in the sun. He raised the iron door knocker and banged once. An orc pulled the door open. Gandul was tempted to hew the orc in half, but resisted the urge, and spoke instead.

"I am here to sign up to be a servant to the Evil Lord." Gandul spoke loudly and clearly, hiding the fear that welled up inside of him.

The orc beckoned Gandul into the castle. When Gandul stepped through the gate into the courtyard, the flowers wilted. The grass died. The castle walls turned from a white marble to a dingy grey granite. The songbirds stopped their singing and turned into crows. And the people walking in the square turned into orcs.

Gandul was then forced to sign a contract,

giving the orcs permission to notify the Evil Lord of his presence at the castle. He was then escorted to the armory where he was suited up in loose chain mail with plate mail on top, and sent to a watchtower to patrol. In a little while an orc came to take his place. Gandul shimmied down the ladder. When he reached the ground he went to search for food. On his way, he heard two orcs talking about a tournament that would happen in four days. The Evil Lord would be fighting first. When Gandul heard about this he grew quite excited and looked forward to attending the festivities.

On the day of the tournament, Gandul entered the tent and was amazed to see how many orcs were there. There were ten thousand of them all waiting to fight in the tournament. Most were wearing plate mail and wielding heavy spiked balls on chains. As Gandul pushed his way to the front of the crowd, an orc announced that the tournament was about to begin. The first person to be called was Gandul; he was to fight the Evil Lord.

Gandul picked up his ax and shield and got into a fighting position. A short figure stepped out of the crowd to face him.

Gandul jumped at the Evil Lord, who swung his morningstar and was about to make contact with Gandul's head, when Gandul swung his shield to block it. The morningstar clipped Gandul's helmet and sent it spinning through the air. Gandul ran to pick up his helmet, but it was too late. All of the orcs had seen that he was a dwarf, not a farmer. The Evil Lord saw, too.

Gandul got to his helmet as the Evil Lord swung

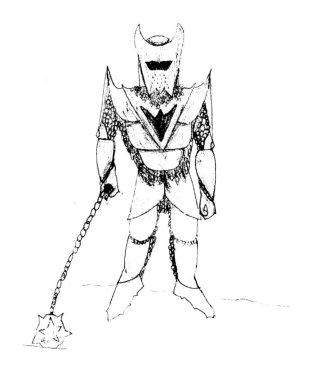

his morningstar. Gandul picked up the helmet and
threw it as hard as he could at his foe. It hit the Evil
Lord's exposed fingers, causing him to drop his
morningstar. Gandul then attacked with his ax, but
the Evil Lord kept blocking his attack. Gandul tripped
him, and, when his enemy hit the ground, Gandul

kicked his helmet off, and saw, to his great dismay, who he had been fighting. He stepped back and dropped his ax, for it was Altor. Altor jumped to his feet and grabbed Gandul's ax.

While Gandul stood gaping, Altor, with an evil grin, sliced off Gandul's head.

ELLA WIEGERS

Excerpt from Memories of a Painting

Museum Visitor

My parents

brought me here to

the museum

I really don't understand their attraction

to large canvases displaying

half-dressed women

their calling sparse black squares

art

we are in London

so why shouldn't we go to interesting

places where normal tourists go

but instead I am being forced to

the Victoria and Albert

the National Gallery

Tate Modern

and the Tate Britain

inside we walk past

Rossetis, Hunts, Millaises

paintings of plots

drawn from myths

poems

legends of old England

maybe it's not so bad

this museum

maybe I'll find

something enjoyable

after all

in the back

of the room

one painting captures my eye

the painting

a woman with

tangled wind-blown hair

the color of dead leaves

an anguished look on her

pale face

dressed in wedding white

a brilliant tapestry

carelessly flung over the

funeral-black side

of her boat

there is something about

the painting

that draws me in

every little detail

the way the tapestry dangles in

the murky water

the erectness of her head

holds my eyes to

the canvas

I wonder their stories

the story shown

the story of the

painting itself

and the stories

of the people

31

who made this art
part of their life

Art Dealer

It isn't my job

to critique

the paintings I sell

but Waterhouse's new picture

is stunning

the subject is fashionable

taken from a poem

by Tennyson

many people have painted

this subject

but this one is different

most Ladies of Shalott

are peaceful

and resigned to their

fate

not this one

her face confronts you

it is anguished but determined

this lady will

not easily give up her

final chance

for happiness

and love

her hopes are all in vain

she will die soon

the season

in the painting is the fall

and the lady is living the autumn

of her life

this painting will sell

I am sure of that

but who will

the lucky

owner

be

Art Critic

I voice my opinions

on art

for a living

most of the time

it is joyless

these days

few paintings are remotely good

the Lady of Shalott

by John William Waterhouse

is spectacular

it steps past

all other Ladies of Shalott

that I have seen

this is no

sugary Hughes

but a masterpiece

it is painted in a way that harkens back to the first

Pre-Raphaelite

pieces

the ones so highly

praised

by my hero Ruskin

I am sure he would enjoy

the realistic autumn light

that streams

onto the dark water

and the way that the

beautifully painted tapestry hangs

over the side of her barge

catching in the stream

but

the paint seems

somehow smeared

in stark contrast to the

pureness of the showing

of the story

the auction tomorrow will

decide

whether the owner will notice any

of this

who knows?

the lucky individual

may love the story

not the technique

E. M. PENROSE

Excerpt from Villainized

PROLOGUE

Lady Zera paced back and forth down the long hallway of the castle and fortress of the evil Lord Valenyx. The walls were decorated with silver and gold, inlaid with red, green, and black gemstones. But despite the beautiful decorations the effect was far from cheerful. The hallway was dark, lit only by candles generously spaced so as to spread light over the largest space. Lady Zera stopped by a mirror. It was in the best lit spot in the hall; candles were placed on each side. For all his strength and power, Lord Valenyx had been a vain man.

Lady Zera slumped against the wall. What should she do now? Lord Valenyx had been killed. Could she count on him being brought back, or were the rumors about him being the son of the Lord of

Death untrue. Was she free? She couldn't think like that. She was Lady Zera, wife of Lord Valenyx, and she was above emotions like this.

Who am I fooling? she thought, glancing into the mirror. Her skin, once so brown, was pale. Her face gaunt. *What have I become?*

CHAPTER 1

Almost thirty years before, a perfect baby girl was born to the wood carver, Alamon, and his wife, Teekà Cepir, in the lovely little village of Sassam. Now in this village it was traditional to take newborns to the fortune-teller to find out which career they were best suited for, who they should study with, and other boring things like that. Interesting fortunes were rare. So it was with much pride that Alamon took his baby to Vecto, who was the current fortune-teller.

Soon he came upon her house, which looked much like a huge, wooden yurt. The house had an ancient and intricately carved door with a metal knocker in the shape of an owl. Alamon knocked three times, the sound echoing through the house.

"Who is it and what do you want?" a husky voice called from inside.

"I am Alamon and I bring my baby girl here for her fortune," Alamon called, grandly.

The door creaked open. Framed in the doorway stood an old woman in a dark green robe with golden trim. She had stature of a much younger woman, though her skin was wrinkled. Alamon felt that one of her eyes didn't work, as if gazing beyond this world.

"Oh, very well then. Come in," Vecto said, rather rudely.

"Thank you," said Alamon, politely.

She grunted in response. Vecto may be an old grump, but her fortunes were almost always right.

Vecto led Alamon to a room cluttered with..."The tools of my trade," she said, waving her hand around in a graceful arch. "I don't use most of them much. But I can't bear to part with them. They have been here since before you were born, boy. Now, let me see the child. Place her in that crib in front of the crystal ball…"

Alamon nodded and did this.

"Go sit in the far corner, there, so that your fortune doesn't interfere with hers."

Alamon sat down on the tiny rickety stool in the corner.

Vecto took one look at the crystal ball then at the baby, gasped, then screamed. Alamon started to get up, then Vecto spoke in a raspy voice:

A child like any other she seems
Yet a monster lurks beneath the surface
Beware the monster, do not release it
If released it will destroy…

She broke off, coughing madly.

"I'm so sorry," she said. "I must have breathed in some dust. Did you say something?"

Alamon, speechless, shook his head.

"Oh, well…I thought I heard…never mind," she said, distractedly. "The crystal ball has never been more unclear on the future of a child. All I can say is that she may have a great many hardships that may make people turn against her. But on the day when all looks lost, she will find hope. None of this is set in stone. She is strong enough to make her own path, but other forces may also be at work to shape her future. The gods are fighting a battle over this one that may shape the world we live in."

Alamon sat stunned at this extraordinary pronouncement.

"Well, anyway," Vecto went on, abruptly returning to earth, "I will write down who she should be apprenticed to. That much of her future *is* clear"

Still dazed, Alamon thanked her as politely as he could.

"It's my job, and I do require payment," was all she said, as she begun looking for some paper.

"What p-payment do you require? I could…uh…make a…a new chair for you to put in the corner instead of that rickety stool?"

"That's fine," said Vecto, waving her hand in an absent-minded way, still searching for a piece of paper.

When Alamon and the baby left she handed Alamon a scroll on which was written the name of the master with whom she should study, and a few other things.

"Zera would be a good name, incidentally," the fortune-teller said, matter-of-factly. Before Alamon could say anything she slammed the door in his face.

He was so preoccupied the rest of that day that he walked right past his house and had to turn around and walk back. Later, after he finally managed to get home, he put the baby in the wood box instead of her crib. She had to cry very loudly to get him to realize his mistake. Then, once he had put the baby in her crib, he tried to cut a hard loaf of bread with a dull butter knife. His wife, noticing his distraction, asked what was wrong, but he wouldn't say. Eventually, Alamon forgot about the prophecy regarding the baby, who they named Zera as the fortune-teller suggested.

• • •

Seven years later, Zera was cooking dinner on their little stove. Teekà had gone to the market. Zera went to the wood box to get more wood for the fire, but it was empty. She ran outside to the woodshed. When she returned, the stove was on fire and flames and smoke had spread throughout the room. Zera stood frozen with shock.

"Zera! ZERA!" Her father grabbed her and pulled her from the house. Fire began to engulf the entire house. "My tools!" gasped Alamon. His tools were inside; they were his only way of making money. If they burned, who knew what would happen to the family.

"Don't go back, Father!" Zera cried, hugging him around the waist, trying to hold him back. "I'll go get your tools!"

"No, Zera!" He pried her off himself easily. "Go to the well for water to throw on the fire."

Zera ran off to the well as Alamon ran back into the house. Smoke filled his lungs, and the heat was unbearable, but still he ran. He grabbed his tools just before part of the burning roof fell onto the shelf where they had been lying. Sparks flew, hitting his face and arms. He waded through the fire as fast as he could. He staggered out of the house just as what was left of the roof fell in. *SPLASH!* Zera had returned from the well and flung a bucketful of water all over him, which put out his clothing, for they had caught fire. Unable to walk, Alamon fell on the grass a few feet from the house and begun to crawl. Zera ran over to him just as people began crowding around with buckets of water to prevent the fire from spreading. Alamon looked awful. His legs were badly burned and his pants were burned to shorts. His arms, face, and chest were speckled with burns from the sparks.

"I'll get more water, Father." She had used all she had collected to stop his clothes from burning.

She ran back to the well, filled the bucket, and hurried back to her father's side. She gave him a drink and tore her apron to make rags which she dipped in the water and placed on his burns.

A boy with long, light brown hair who was hardly older than Zera helped her by getting more water. He was very nice.

"My name is Dmitri, by the way," he said with an easy smile.

"I'm Zera, and this is my father, Alamon."

Just then Teekà arrived.

"What happened?"

"Fire," Alamon said in a croaky voice.

"Well, I can see that! How did it start? Did you get anything out?"

"Father risked his life to get his tools out. His legs are badly burned," Zera said.

"How did it start?" Teekà asked again.

Zera, who had been holding back tears the whole time, began to cry. She hugged her legs to her chest and put her head on her knees

Not knowing what to do, Dmitri ran back to the well again to get her some water to drink.

"Zera, what happened?" The sharpness in her mother's voice made her cry harder. Teekà had never used that tone with her before. "Zera, stop that and tell me what happened!" Her mother grabbed one of Zera's arms and attempted to pull her to her feet.

The crowd of people, having reduced the fire to mostly smoldering ash, began to gather around Alamon, Teekà, and Zera. Some were saying things like: "Teekà, calm down," and, "Don't yell at her like that!"

"She had something to do with my house burning to the ground!" Teekà screamed. "Zera, get up and tell me what you have done!" But, having been released from her mother's clutches, Zera just sat on the ground and cried.

"Fine," said Teekà. "If you won't admit to what you have done, then go away. I never want to see you again."

Zera sobbed even harder. Alamon raised his

hand and placed it on her shoulder.

"I...love...you...Zera," was all he said. His hand fell to the ground.

"Father?" her voice trembled. "PAPA!" She shook him. "Papa, wake up! PAPA!"

"You can't wake him now," said a man in the crowd. He was tall with messy blonde hair. Many would have called him handsome, but there was something not quite right in his eyes. They were blue, but they looked fogged over. "I think he's dead."

"Leave!" Teekà commanded. "Go away, you useless child! Now look what you have done! You killed your own father!"

Some of the fog seemed to clear from the eyes of the man in the crowd, he stepped forward.

"I can care for her until she has somewhere else to go," he said.

"Who are you?" Teekà said, rudely.

"My name is Rian Armondo Zee. I live just down the street there," he said pointing. "I will let her stay in my house, and I will feed her until she has a teacher. If you don't mind." He was very polite.

"And where will you find a teacher for this worthless child?" Teekà asked.

"If no one will have her, then I will teach her myself. Who did the fortune-teller say she should be apprenticed to?"

"How should I know? I'm sure the paper was burned along with everything else in my house." She added a nasty look at Zera, who was still on the ground weeping.

"You," Rian said, "are not the only one who had losses today. Zera and I will be going now."

He bent to pick her up just as a wind came up. A piece of paper fluttered through the air and landed at Zera's feet. It was charred, but read quite clearly:

Ival Festo, Professor of Magic

RUEVEAR
Waffles

Illustrated by the author

Once upon a time there was a dragon named Waffles. He was the most colorful dragon on Saturn. He was part unicorn, plant-eating dinosaur, cat, and Chinese dragon.

He was not like other dragons. He was not mighty or fearsome. He was kind, caring, and clever. For example, he loved making marzipan figures.

Waffles went to a regular public school, where the other dragons thought he was odd.

One day he was so sick of having no friends, he painted himself red and his horn white so he looked like the other dragons.

It worked till his paint started to wear off. Then they all laughed at him.

The next plan was to put a bed sheet over his body and cut holes for his eyes. That didn't work because his horn was sharp and tore a hole in it. They just made fun of him more.

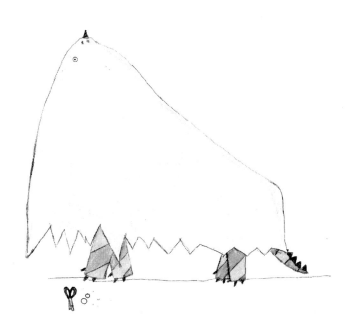

Finally he decided he would go to the spring dragon dance where he would just be himself. When he showed up, everyone stared, then carried on with their fun. He looked around and saw a girl dragon, and thought he would say hello. She was different, too. She was purple with huge green eyes.

He asked her, "You lonely?"

"Yes, a little bit," she said in a sad tone. "I get left out because I'm different."

"I'm the same way," Waffles said. "No one treats me the same as the other dragons."

"My name is Luna. What's yours?"

"I'm Waffles. What is your favorite thing to do?"

"My favorite thing to do is to make marzipan in all shapes, sizes, and colors," said Luna.

"Me, too. It's also my favorite candy," said Waffles.

After they talked awhile, they decided they would go make marzipan. During that time they found they had many similarities, like roller-skating, writing, and dancing. They became a great team and always had each other's backs.

ODETTE JENNINGS

Excerpt from Red Creek

The early summer morning promised nothing but the expected: an early wakeup, a hasty breakfast, clothes put on quickly, and hair forgotten to be brushed. Skipping out the door, I couldn't help but notice the heat of the morning. As I walked down the road, I hardly knew where I was going. I most definitely prefer it that way, however. If you walk with a purpose the only thing you can focus on is your purpose. Let's say you're walking to get an ice cream. As you walk, does anything cross your mind besides the ice cream? Or perhaps how you wish you had decided to bike, or could walk faster?

After I made my loop around the neighborhood, I came back around to my house. The grass was unnaturally green and perky, considering the weather, but the flowers were starting to fade. The house was almost all the way to the end of the street, just far enough away for me to walk all the way down to the main road and back before I started to die of heat exhaustion. The paint on the picket fence was chipping and the pathway had cracks in it. I sat down on the couch and closed my eyes. I could hear from the other room the radio my mother must have forgotten to turn off. The radio was kept against the far wall in the corner of her sewing room and took up a lot of space. It looked a bit like a big square table, except for the controls on the front. My mother had a lace tablecloth draped over it and set some of her supplies on top.

Mother didn't usually let me listen to the news, so I turned it down low and pressed my ear up against the speaker. Maybe I would have my own radio station someday.

The static was louder than the man's voice I heard in the background. I opened my journal. In the upper right corner I etched the elegant signature I had been working on: the *F* swooped down in a curl, and the tail of the *e* twirled around and back, creating a figure-eight-like shape. Below it, I wrote the date: July 12, 1916. Dissatisfied with the loop of my *2,* I erased it and rewrote a much more pleasing version.

Suddenly, a word registered in my mind. *Shark.* Where had it come from? And then I heard it again. *"People fled from the beaches as a young man was brought ashore after a brutal attack. Could it have been a shark?"* I dropped my pen. The words echoed in my mind. I turned up the volume and listened for more.

The door clicked as my mother shut it behind her.

"Florence!" she called.

I quickly shut off the radio.

"In here, Mother!"

She entered with her arms full of groceries and layers of clothing she must have peeled off in the day's heat.

"Would you help me, darling?"

I got up from the couch, took a bag of groceries

from her arms, and headed to the kitchen.

• • •

Keeping a secret can be difficult, especially for me. I pride myself in my honesty, but sometimes I wish I weren't so honest. That night at the dinner table I was waiting for the moment when my mother would bring up the big issue on the news, but that moment never came.

After being excused from the dinner table, I snuck back into the sewing room and switched on the radio. The static wasn't as bad as it had been before so I could almost make out every word the man was saying.

"A shark scare reported earlier has been proven false. Scientists have examined the body and now blame the attacks on a large killer whale."

• • •

The doorbell rang at six o'clock sharp and I rushed to answer it like a dog rushing to be fed. Tonight's dinner was going to be one of the best yet. Of course, this wasn't because of the food, but rather, the guests. My cousin, Henry, had been gone for the entire weekend on a family vacation to the beach. My parents were forced to stay behind with me because I am allergic to the beach. Technically, I'm not allergic, but I wish I were because that would give me a perfect excuse to never go near those sticky, hot places called beaches.

I flung open the door with a smile and invited them in. My aunt and uncle rushed inside to say hello to my parents, but Henry remained in the doorway. The look of him was off, to say the least. When he finally lifted his head and looked at me, his eyes brightened and he quickly came inside. I closed the door behind him and stood there waiting for an explanation, or at least a greeting.

"Flo, I need to talk to you," he murmured under his breath. His dark eyebrows were tangled and twisted and his forehead had a deep crease down the center. I nodded and we walked to my room and sat down on my bed.

"Have you...uh...heard anything about...I don't know...have you listened to the news at all lately?" His voice was so small I had to strain to hear it.

"Yeah, I listened to my mother's radio while she was running errands." I giggled a childish giggle and immediately regretted it.

"It was late at night when the man was attacked," Henry said. "He was out swimming by himself and there was no one on the beach; everyone had gone in for the night. I went in, too, with my family, but as we were walking in, I remembered that I had left my shoes on the beach. Since it wasn't too dark out yet, they let me run back to get them, if I promised to be quick. While I was there I saw the man out swimming. He was far away, but I saw him."

He paused to wipe the sweat from his forehead, then looked up at me for a second. I nodded for him to continue.

"He was swimming really fast and was heading the opposite direction of the beach. The water was completely still. I knew I should be heading back soon so that my parents wouldn't worry, but then out of the corner of my eye I saw it."

"Saw what?"

He just looked down and pressed his pointer finger against his temple.

"Saw what?" I asked again.

"A shark."

"Haven't you heard the news? They're saying it was a killer whale."

"Yes, I heard it. I am telling you I saw a shark attack that man."

Could this really be happening? Finally the excitement I had been hoping for?

"I want to believe you. But I don't know if I can," I croaked.

• • •

Sitting at the dinner table that night was quite the challenge. I quickly began to tire of the silence mixed with the occasional clinking of silverware. I wished for someone to please just say something, anything. I knew the reason, of course. I knew they were mad at Henry for claiming he saw a shark, and I knew they wouldn't even bring up their weekend at the beach for fear of mentioning the attack.

People didn't think sharks were dangerous, and the idea that one attacked a human was just too scary for anyone to believe. A man once jumped into water infested with sharks to prove they were harmless, and he escaped without a scratch. He even offered a reward to anyone who could prove that a shark had ever attacked a man, and no one could. Henry and I probably weren't the only people who believed that sharks were dangerous, but no one else was admitting it.

If Henry told his parents what he saw, they wouldn't believe him for a second. They would probably think he had gone mad. But I could tell he had told them.

When everyone was finished eating, I jumped up to clear the table. I knew Henry was upset that I didn't believe him. I wished that I could. Mother offered dessert and they all politely said they were too full from dinner: my Mother's delicious roasted chicken, but also vegetables that tasted like mush, which I was forced to eat. Maybe I'm terrible at lying, but I certainly can detect it. I knew my mother was hurt. She was a wonderful hostess, but failed to hide her disappointment behind the fake smile plastered on her face.

She showed Henry the door and thanked them for coming.

"Florence!" my mother called from the kitchen.

"Yes?"

"Why don't you head to bed, dear. I'll be up in a minute."

She didn't like me around when she was upset, which explained why she was sending me to bed at eight o'clock. She kissed me on the forehead and I walked down the hallway and up the stairs to my bedroom. A stack of neatly folded clothes were on my bed. Everything my mother did was filled with neatness.

After my mom tucked me in, she left the room, turned off the light, and shut the door. I tiptoed out of bed cautiously and rummaged through my desk drawers until I found my journal. It opened to a blank page. I sat at my desk and undid my hair, letting it fall over my shoulders. I got out my favorite pen and drew a picture of Henry on the beach. His feet were waded into the water and his smile stretched almost all the way across his face. Aunt Margaret was sitting on a beach towel with an umbrella to shade her from the sun. She wore a red-and-white striped bathing suit with ruffles around the hem. Her hand was up in the air waving at Henry, and he was twisted around waving back at her. I drew the sun high in the sky and the water a deep, saturated blue. There were many other people scattered throughout the water: splashing each other, swimming, talking. But there was one young man who had ventured farther than the rest. So far that you could barely see his arm peeking out of the water as he swam away from the shore. My final touch was a dark gray fin piercing through the water like the blade of a sharp knife. I circled the fin, pressing down so hard that I made a dent in the paper. I wrote next to it, *Does this look like a killer whale to you?* I tore it out of my journal, folded it into thirds, and hid it in the back of my desk drawer.

Omm

O. J. R. WEINBLATT DEY
Excerpt from The Uniter

Illustrated by the author

The cobblestone road wound through Theliforn village like a never-ending snake. The light breeze sent ripples through the tall green grass. The bright yellowish-white suns streamed into the boy's eyes. Upon Canule Hill, overlooking the village, sat Eloth Ba'nush, a boy about the age of fourteen. His boney face was smudged with mud and dirt. He was tall and slender with a small but straight nose. His eyes were the color of dark grass and his hair, amber. He wore a pullover, dark green, long-sleeved shirt made of lox wool. A small brown satchel hung down to his thighs. He wore his brown lox leather pants that had been gifted to him from his uncle Feorlon, the only relative Eloth knew. The pair of pants were his most prized piece of clothing, as they were very useful for doing

all the hard work.

Eloth had volunteered to herd lox a few years back; it was a tough job, and a big responsibility, but his mom, Gwendell, thought he could keep a safe eye on them. Lox are large animals, with small horns and beady eyes. They have rough, dark tan hair, cloven hooves, and a very strong skull for protection when bucking. Eloth had to take the lox out in the morning, feed them, and watch them roam through the damp fields the rest of the day. In the evening, Eloth would herd the lox back in, feed them once more, and lead them back to their sleeping dens. Though it was Eloth's choice to herd the lox, he would much rather be with his friend, Zemm, a boy less than a year younger than he was. He had to help his mom make more Ploom, their kind of money, so he could still have a home and be fed by his mother.

Eloth was nine and Zemm, eight, when Zemm had nearly been trampled dead by two men from some foreign place. They wore silvery armor and long green capes. A voltry metal sword swayed back and forth on their sides. The men rode on white hairy creatures with large twisted horns and powerful hooves. Zemm had been in gratitude ever since. Eloth was never that good at making friends; he had never had one before Zemm.

While Eloth sat on Canule Hill, he marveled at his surroundings. Not because he had not seen them before, but because he loved nature. And it was not always nice out, with the climate they lived in. Eloth grew up around all the plants, the bushes, the trees. The methlon tree sprouts yellow flowers all over the branches and produces a succulent pink fruit that only grows in the spring. The denluve tree has no fruit or flowers at all, just two-inch-long spikes covering every part of the tree. You could tell by its looks that it was a tree you would not want to climb. The leafy oo'muk tree could grow up to fifty feet high. The bushy leaves sprouted down low, making it perfect for a game of Ketts.

Ketts was a rough game that required eight players, four for each team. One team was named the

Ketts and the other was named the Coons. The Ketts hid in the best place they could find within one minute, but it needed to be a good place for escaping, too. If a Coon spotted a Kett, the Kett would run, but if the Coon tackled him, he would be taken to the Coons' jail. If the Kett could break out of the Coon's grasp before being put in jail, he would run to find another hiding spot. The Coons won the game if all the Ketts were in their jail. The Ketts won if the thirty-minute time limit was up and none of them were in jail.

One month ago, the farmers had harvested all the methlon fruit. Eloth and Zemm did not like that they were not allowed to have the fruit. The farmers said that it was the property of the village and it would be a crime to take some. They might have taken a few but they did not call that stealing. The farmers found the trees; they did not plant them.

Gwendell told them, "'Tis just business."

"Cheating business," Zemm would say, jokingly.

After the harvest, the farmers would sell half of the fruit, and dry the other half to keep and sell through the rest of the year.

Eloth sat on the hill, smiling curiously, as he wondered what his father was like. Was he funny or was he serious? Maybe he was playful, but he might have been calm. He had left when Eloth was just an infant. Eloth had never been told why. Gwendell would not say anything when he asked, except, "Your father was a good man." Then she would trudge off sternly.

A voice startled him from his daydream on the hill.

"Kaphelo!" the young boy's voice called happily. Eloth looked to see Zemm skipping up the hill. Kaphelo is a kind of large bird, its dark red feathers appear black at night, which helps them camouflage to catch their prey. It was Eloth's birth name; each child would get an animal birth name before their real one.

"Tintag!" Eloth replied, running to hug Zemm.

A Tintag is a deer-sized creature with ten-inch long horns. It has short black fur and cloven hooves. It is an herbivore and a very good jumper. Eloth and Zemm still used the names for fun.

"What are you doing up here?" Eloth asked, surprised by how loud he said it.

"There is no need to yell," Zemm replied, laughing.

"Very sorry, sir," Eloth joked.

"Decided I would come see you. I am free from working at the market for today, and I wanted to say good-bye before I left to see my grandmother."

"Well, a good decision, I say."

"What do you do up on a hill?" Zemm asked.

"Think, enjoy the day—that is what I do," Eloth said.

"You are lucky you can 'enjoy the day.' I have to work at the market," Zemm said with an annoyed voice.

"The market is a great place, but you have got to know the things to do. First thing, always bring a few ploom. My favorite stand is probably that one with all the jarred animals. I have a few of those at home."

"I never get let off work."

"It used to be like that for me, but I made a trade with my mom. I do extra work around the house, but it is worth it."

Eloth and Zemm talked for some time, on and on, about what they had planned for the week.

"I am working. My uncle, Feorlon, shall arrive in two days, that is all I know," Eloth said.

"I will be at my grandmother's house for five days and then back home," Zemm said.

They talked awhile more, but Eloth had to herd lox and Zemm had to work.

"I should be off. I have packing to do and you have work," Zemm said drowsily.

"'Twas nice to see you," Eloth said with a smile.

"'Twas, Eloth," Zemm replied.

He ran back down Canule Hill, across the

grassy field, through the lox fences, and on to the cobblestone road leading into the village.

The light in the sky was now less than before. The two suns were setting in the west and north. Eloth got lazily to his feet and counted the number of lox to see if any had strayed from the pack. This was a big fear of Eloth's. If he did not keep a good enough eye on them and one went missing, he would be to blame. He called them by name, then led the lox into their fences, fed them the mixture of theen grass and quan root, then brought them to their dens.

Eloth jogged into the village and through the cabins with thatched roofs. He stopped at a little house, with a wood-woven door made of the small, bendy Wila'wong bush. One window was on the left side of the cabin. Eloth stepped inside the cabin, walked through the hallway and into the small room. On the right, there was a round table with three chairs. Farther back, there sat a bed big enough for two; Gwendell slept in that one. To the left, there was a ladder leading up to a loft. The loft's floor was covered in lox skins and a few knit blankets; Eloth slept up there. There was a shelf that had two jarred animals on it, and a stick with a crosspiece tied to it that Eloth used as a play sword, and a piece of parchment with a picture he had drawn when he was little. There was a small stone fireplace on the wall with a small flame lit in the middle of it; Gwendell sat by it, knitting silently. On the right was a desk with a quill and ink. A bucket of parchment sat there. A small book shelf stood by the desk. Eloth's favorite book, when he was five, was "Saroon and the Voltry Noox." Eloth now kept a small journal in his satchel, along with a small quill and ink bottle, and a few rusty pins.

"Hello, Mother," Eloth said.

"Hello, dear," Gwendell said calmly without looking up at him.

"What may be for dinner, Mother?" Eloth asked.

"I did not make dinner, for I am saving our supply of food for when Feorlon arrives, but I do have a chunk of lox cheese and a wood-apple," Gwendell said as if Eloth was not there.

Lox cheese is white and very creamy with a slight tang to the tongue. As for wood-apple, it is a soft and very sweet fruit the color of a dark red sunset.

"That will do, Mother, thank you," Eloth said with a sigh.

Eloth spoke politely to his elders, especially his mother. It was said that if you did not show the elders the respect they deserved, the spirits of the four winds would curse you until you changed, but it was all a myth. Eloth did not believe it really, but was polite anyway.

After Eloth had finished his light meal, he climbed up to the loft. He pried up a loose floorboard, and pulled out a giant book. He used it to teach himself fascinating words. Gwendell used to teach him because school was too much to pay for, but as Eloth grew older, he had to start teaching himself. He looked at the book until his eyelids grew heavy, and he fell asleep with the large book on his belly, slowly rising up, and sinking down.

It was dim and musky outside. The light drops of dew could be heard faintly outside the cabin. Small slivers of each sun peaked over the horizon. Eloth rubbed his eyes then peered through his boney fingers. He stood up; his legs were sore and shaky. He climbed slowly down the ladder, sometimes missing a rung and almost falling to the ground.

"You look awfully slow this morning, dear," Gwendell said happily, washing a metal plate in a bucketful of water.

"My guess is…ahh…work, Mother," Eloth said weakly. He made grunting sounds as he walked across the floor.

"You will be sore all over at my age," Gwendell said with a laugh.

"Mother…eh…you are at the age of thirty-eight," Eloth said rubbing his legs as gently as he could.

"I could have been a little more active in my

younger days," Gwendell said with a frown.

"You think you can still accompany me to the market?" Gwendell asked.

"YES!" Eloth screeched.

"Would you be calm, Eloth? I was NOT going to say no."

"Sorry, Mother," Eloth said, grinding his teeth.

The people in the market swarmed like bees coming and going from their hive. Eloth helped his mother carry a few sacks full of clothes she had knit. He tried to get people to buy the knit hats, scarves, sweaters, and slippers, but it was not the time of year to sell warm clothing.

Eloth finally was let off duty. It was a good feeling when he did not have a task to do, so he would admire the market and all its beauty. With a few ploom in his pocket, Eloth skipped through the market kicking up dust as he went. He looked at all the bizarre and interesting things, from potions to jarred Vonik fishes.

He squeezed through a couple of small crowds

that were clumped around unseeable stands.

"You there, chap!" said a snappy voice once

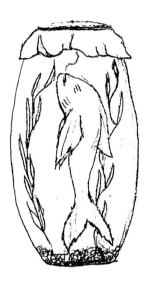

Eloth was out of the crowd.

Eloth looked to see where the voice had come from. He saw a squat man with a black beard covered in pendants.

"Boy, is your brain working?" the man asked speaking again.

"Yes, yes, sir!" Eloth said after he could come to his senses from admiring the peculiar little man.

"Ah, he has manners as well as looks," the small man said with a smile. "My name is Wethul Runth. What be yours, young laddie?"

"Eloth Ba'nush, sir."

"Oh, do not call me 'sir.' If anybody is calling anybody 'sir,' it should be me saying it to you!" Wethul exclaimed.

"Sorry," Eloth posed, "Wethul."

"Do not apologize for that my boy, but do buy one of my necklaces. They are lucky charms," he said dramatically.

"I guess I could buy one," Eloth thought, to be nice to Wethul.

"Good good, how about this one," Wethul said holding out a small glass container with nothing in it. It was attached to a leather strap.

"I will take it and put something in it," Eloth said, putting out his hand.

"Do not put something in it, but that'll be five ploom," Wethul said, insistently.

"Okay," Eloth said, scratching his head.

Eloth fumbled around in his pocket, then pulled out five silver coins the size of his big toenail. Eloth and Wethul exchanged the items.

"Thank you, farewell," they said to each other as Eloth walked away.

Eloth had to get back to work. In the past Gwendell had not been too happy when he was late; she would always say, "Quick is the trick," and make him work a little bit harder. He walked speedily through the vendor stands, occasionally bumping into someone. It seemed to be especially busy today. Eloth only went twice a week, but he had never seen it this crowded. For being such a small village, it was unusual that Theliforn market was so famous, but still people would take long journeys through the forest surrounding the village to see it.

Eloth scanned the buildings for some way to climb up on the roofs so he could avoid the clumps of people. He saw a stack of barrels leaned against a cabin. They were cracked all over, so he had to be cautious when climbing. Eloth slipped behind a stand, then over to the barrels. He stepped on the first one, then on the second, grabbed the rim of the roof, then CRACK! The barrel split in half. Hundreds of wood apples dropped to the ground. Eloth hoisted himself to the roof and lay flat on his back. By now all the people in the area had looked that way to see what had happened. Shouts of disappointment came from the owner who sold the produce.

"I knew I should never have used those damn barrels!" the high voice cursed.

Eloth tried to keep still. He held his breath and hoped none saw him. He waited some time, then finally peeked over the edge of the roof. There were dark red splotches all over the ground where the wood apples had fallen.

Eloth kept low as he sneaked across the roofs. He could see his mother's stand. While looking for a way down, Eloth heard shouts from someone in the market.

"Somebody stop him!"

A man holding a white embroidered purse came

into sight. He was running away from something or someone, but soon it became clear to Eloth what he was running from. A young woman appeared and chased after him.

"He stole my purse! HELP!"

Eloth watched as the crowds parted. The thief was almost to the archway. A slender man who looked about sixty-five stepped into the path. He had a short, grey beard and wore a maroon robe with a golden lining.

"Get out of my way, old man!" the thief yelled, and drew a knife.

For a second, Eloth thought he saw a flicker in the bearded man's eyes.

Just then the thief flew backwards and slammed to the ground. A circle of dust lifted around the robber. Gasps rose up from the crowds surrounding the scene. After two men came and grabbed the thief, the old man's eyes fixed upon Eloth atop the roof.

You better get down before somebody sees you boy, a calm voice said in Eloth's head. He looked at the old man, confused. The bearded man smiled at him, than slipped into the crowd.

"Uncle Feorlon shall be arriving tomorrow afternoon," Gwendell said to Eloth as they walked back from the market.

"Yes, mother, how could I forget?" Eloth said, but his mind was in a different place; he was thinking about the old man.

At home, Eloth walked straight to the ladder leading up to the loft.

"And where do you think you are going, Eloth?" Gwendell said, strictly.

"To bed, mother," Eloth replied, plainly.

"It's nearly six o'clock and you have not had dinner."

Eloth paused. "Oh, right, dinner."

"C'mon then, Eloth, to the table."

Eloth had trouble sleeping that night because of his excitement to see Feorlon. But the excitement he had could not hold his eyelids open the whole night. Eventually, he fell asleep.

He awoke to find that it was still dark. He tried to go back to sleep, but the thought of it seemed almost impossible.

Light finally arrived. It was as if the whole land had turned golden. Rays of sun showed all the dust particles floating in the room. Eloth jumped up, bolted down the ladder, grabbed his coat, and ran out the door to feed the lox and let them out.

"Eloth," Gwendell called after him, "Your breakfast."

He ran back through the door. "Yes mother, how could I forget," he said, as he snatched the piece of Monnith bread from the table and sprinted back out the door.

Eloth kept giving quick glances to the opening of the forest where the dirt road wound into the village. He watched the lox lazily roam around the wet grass groaning to each other, then back to the road to look for his uncle.

It was now half past twelve, but still no sign of Feorlon. Eloth saw a hooded figure on a tompa ride into view. A tompa is a round, stumpy mammal with big bulgy eyes. They can run very fast if they want. Eloth knew the funny beast was Vilgo, Feorlon's pet.

"Uncle!" Eloth called from across the field. He sprinted through the damp grass and into Feorlon's outstretched arms.

"Eloth my boy! You have grown so much since last we met. And Gwendell, how is she?" Feorlon asked with concern.

"Better than you could imagine!" Eloth said with excitement.

"Good, I would not want my nephew stressing about things. Eloth, watch the lox. That one is looking towards the trees," he said, pointing to one of the scruffy-haired creatures.

"Well, see you at dinner. Ronna, come here," Eloth said, jogging over to the lox.

Eloth skipped through the village, happily. He imagined what was for dinner, maybe lox chops seasoned with pemga spice, or maybe oslo, a rabbit-sized white mammal with big ears, and a big snout, and a short tail. Eloth then realized he had missed his cabin. He turned around and walked back. Eloth

opened the door to the small structure and stepped inside.

"You're late Eloth," Gwendell said with strict tone in her voice.

"Sorry, Mother, I, um, I walked past the cabin," he said, nervously wondering what she would think of his reply.

She looked at Eloth in confusion, "Well, sit down, it will not do any good to stand there. Here, serve yourself some lox and gwanda dumpling soup."

Eloth smiled at Feorlon as he walked to the table. He ate the soup loudly with large slurps.

"So, Eloth," Feorlon said once Eloth had drank all the broth, "how are you enjoying life?"

"I am living it as fully as possible," Eloth said happily, as he finished his last bites of soup.

"I am glad, 'tis no small thing to live a life," Feorlon said with a yawn.

Hours passed by as they talked, but eventually it was time to rest their tired heads.

Eloth climbed up the ladder, Feorlon following behind.

"Sleep well, Eloth," Feorlon said as he lay down.

"Can I ask you a question?" Eloth asked.

"Ask away," Feorlon replied.

"My father…why did he leave us?" Eloth asked, swallowing the lump in his throat.

"I wish I could tell you, but I do not know. Wherever he is, he thinks of you every day…" Feorlon started.

"So you think he is still alive?" Eloth interrupted.

"I will do anything to believe my little brother is

still alive, but I know he loves you dearly and is trying to get back to his home with Gwendell and you," Feorlon said, closing his eyes.

"Thank you, Uncle," Eloth said, with a hint of a smile.

•　•　•

Eloth awoke that morning with a cramp in his neck.

He climbed down the ladder and onto the floor.

"You are up early this morning, Eloth," Gwendell said, eating a wood-apple.

"Neck cramp. Must have been how I slept," Eloth said, blinking his eyes.

"Here, I have some tunto oil. Come, it will help ease the pain," Gwendell said, taking a metal container from a shelf.

"Where is Uncle Feorlon, Mother?" Eloth asked, wondering why he was not in the cabin.

"He said he was off to the blacksmith to pick up something he had ordered yesterday," Gwendell said, rubbing the oil into the back of Eloth's neck.

"All right. May I visit Mister Thornbuckle, Mother?" Eloth asked anxiously.

"May I ask why?" Gwendell said, with suspicion.

"Questions that have been getting to the back of my head, Mother, questions only he can answer, that is all," Eloth said, grinning mischievously.

"Very well, then, but if I catch you not telling me the truth, you will not be happy," she said with a glare.

● ● ●

Eloth walked with small steps on the cobblestone road. He walked past cabins of all different shapes and sizes. Some were round and short, some were tall and skinny, some were even long with three different floors.

Eloth came to a big, round cabin with two floors. He nervously stepped up to the door, grabbed the

93

yulak metal knocker, and banged twice.

The door to the cabin slowly opened. A grey-haired man peeked out from inside.

"Oh, hello, my dear, what brings you here?" the old man asked.

"Hello, Mister Thornbuckle," Eloth said politely. "I have came to ask you a question."

"Well, come in, please, as it will not do any good to just stand there," Mr. Thornbuckle said.

"Thank you, sir," Eloth said with a smile.

"Ah, Eloth, you mother did teach you very well," Mr. Thornbuckle replied, sounding pleased.

Eloth stepped into the house. The walls were dark brown, made from mud, and had a glossy finish so they looked nicer. There was a lox-skin sofa and chair with a small rowg-wood table in the middle of the room.

"Sit here and make yourself at home," Mr. Thornbuckle said, showing Eloth the sofa. "Would you like some lox cheese and empur-root tea? I just made a pot of it!"

"I would love some, thank you," Eloth said, licking his lips.

Empur-root tea was a delicacy in that part of the land, mostly because empur-root did not grow in those parts. Mr. Thornbuckle went to the kitchen to prepare the lox cheese and pour the tea, then returned.

"Here we are," Mr. Thornbuckle said, bringing out a yulak metal platter with two cups made of painted rowg-wood, plus a half block of lox cheese. "Now, what was your question?"

"Uh," Eloth said, uncertainly, "do you know why my father left?"

"So you were finally brave enough to ask. All those times, had you really come only to have the tea and cheese?" Mr. Thornbuckle asked, as if he were expecting that question.

"No, sir," Eloth said in shame.

"No shame in that, no shame in that!" Mr. Thornbuckle said, with understanding in his voice.

"But back to your question. Your father was an honorable man. Surprisingly, I even remember when he would come and visit me as a child."

Eloth smiled at the thought of it.

"It is a matter of respect, Eloth, my boy, when you visit an elder; it is said to give good luck. But, Eloth, your father had a gift, a very special gift," Mr. Thornbuckle said in a hush.

"What do you mean by gift?" Eloth asked.

"I am sure you will find out soon. I would like you to stay, but I have some important work to do," Mr. Thornbuckle said, changing the subject.

Eloth got up and walked over to the door. "But..." he began.

"Enjoy the sun while it is still here, my boy," Mr. Thornbuckle interrupted, then closed the door in Eloth's face.

"How can I enjoy the sun when I still want to know the answer to my question?" Eloth asked himself angrily as he walked away.

• • •

Eloth walked through the door of the small cabin, and went over to the chair by the furnace and slumped down in it.

"Hello, Eloth," Gwendell said getting up from her bed.

"Hello, Mother," Eloth said moodily.

"You do not look too happy, Eloth, dear. Please tell me what is wrong," she begged.

"Why would you want to know?" Eloth replied harshly.

"I am your mother, Eloth. I want to know so I can help you, dear," Gwendell said, hugging Eloth.

"You never want to talk, Mother, at least not about how I am doing or how I feel!" Eloth said angrily.

"Eloth, you are overreacting. Now what is the matter?" Gwendell asked.

"I was asking about Father. Why have you never told me anything about him?" Eloth asked.

"Because, Eloth, I do not know why he left. All I know is that he was a great man and that is why I married him," Gwendell said, and got up from her crocheting position.

Just then, Feorlon walked through the door with his hands behind his back.

"Eloth, I have something for you," he said in a tempting voice.

Eloth jumped out of the chair in excitement, forgetting the upsetting feeling he had had a moment ago.

"This is no toy to fool with," Feorlon warned Eloth, then he took out a long object rapped in a piece linith cloth.

"What is it, Uncle?" Eloth asked with curiosity.

"I guess you will just have to find out," Feorlon said, handing him the gift.

Eloth opened the cloth, revealing a dagger. His eyes widened with surprise. The dagger's blade was about a foot long, made of aldith metal. The hilt was a dark wood called welsop. The grip was made of lox leather.

"Thank you, thank you, Uncle!" Eloth

exclaimed gripping the dagger firmly in his hand.

"I thought it might be time, but, Eloth, remember only use it if you are threatened. It is no toy, understand?" Feorlon asked wisely.

"Yes, Uncle, I understand," Eloth said, though his heart pounded with excitement to use it right away.

"He really had to talk me into letting you have a weapon, Eloth, so be grateful you have this," Gwendell said proudly.

"Yes mother," Eloth said, still looking down at the dagger.

For the rest of the day, Eloth played with his dagger carefully and away from people. He knew that he was not strong enough to block a full grown man's attack, so he had to use his agility to defeat his opponents in combat. But what was he thinking? He knew he never would fight. What was the likelihood of him actually facing an opponent? If anything, he would be fighting an animal of some sort. A small one.

Eloth strapped his dagger to his lox leather pants, and ran back home before anyone found out he had been whacking down flowers with his weapon.

STORY WALSH

Living Things

In the middle of the night when everyone's asleep.

And everyone's in bed, not making a peep.

Well, I hope you believe me, because it's really true.

The only thing that's moving happens to be a shoe.

"Come out," he cries, his voice full of joy.

Now two things are stirring, a shoe and a toy.

Objects begin to shuffle, things like a guitar.

Then something begins beeping, and it might be a car.

And then the beeping turns into a clatter and a bang.

Footsteps are thumping loudly; the spade utters, "Oh, dang."

"We'd better play dead," the desk whispers out.

And then three seconds later there comes a loud shout.

"WHO LEFT OUT THESE LEGOS!" the man bellows with a groan.

"AND WHAT IS THIS THAT'S ON THE

GROUND? COULD IT BE THE TELEPHONE?"

The man turns on the lamp, with a big mighty glare,

and lets out a roar louder than a bear.

"JIMMY, COME DOWN HERE AND PICK UP ALL THIS MESS!

WILL YOU BE IN TROUBLE? OH, YOU JUST WAIT AND GUESS!"

A little boy entered the room, no more than six years old.

"NEXT TIME, JIMMY, OH, YOU'D BETTER DO WHAT YOU ARE TOLD!"

A slap to the face is all it takes to get the objects riled up.

He's attacked in a cluster of pencils, books, and a sled.

And in a few minutes the man's lying dead.

The little boy's eyes are widened with fright.

Then the briefcase utters, "Well, he didn't fight."

The little boy jumps up and lets out a cheer.

"Thank you, oh, thank you! I won't live in fear."

And so they lived happily—shoe, desk, boy, and

spade.

And never again did the boy need any aid.

RUEVEAR

Excerpt from Zanika's Island

Under the tree, we looked at Scott's wound and saw that it was really inflamed. Scott was crying, not so much from the pain as from the shock. I was sure it did hurt. The arrow went straight through Scott's hand; only the feathers were left sticking to the blood that was still oozing from the wound. Scott was losing a lot of blood, and we were scared that he might die.

Thankfully a girl came into sight. She had bright green eyes and short blonde hair done up in pigtails. She was jumping her way down the rocks on the hill in front of us.

She paused for a moment. "Are you guys okay? I was just trying to scare you away, but I saw that I hit your friend in the hand," she said.

"He is our brother, and he is badly hurt, thanks to you! We need your help," I said.

My sister, Rinay, asked, "What is your name?"

"My name is Artemis," she said as she hopped off the bottom rock and rushed to Scott. She reached into her messenger bag and pulled out a first aid kit and her pliers. She opened the metal box and took out tweezers. She used the tweezers to pluck out the feathers from Scott's wound, and used the pliers to pull out the arrow. Then she took out hydrogen peroxide and carefully cleaned the wound, and applied direct pressure to stop the bleeding. Rinay and I cringed as Scott screamed out in pain. Soon, Artemis put a gauze bandage on his gash to keep it clean and disinfected. Scott began to calm down from the arnica root Artemis gave him.

"You guys should probably stay at my place, until you build your own, but first I need to learn your names," said Artemis.

"I am Leon," I said.

"I am Rinay. We mentioned our brother's name is Scott."

"Groovy. I guess you guys can follow me to my

home now. It is a little ways, though we probably will get there in about thirty minutes," Artemis said.

We all stood up and followed her in a line over the rocks and through the river and trees to her home. Her house was about a thousand steps up from where we had started.

Scott's agony had reached the point where he was screaming and becoming a little bit tipsy and falling asleep while scream-walking. Rinay and I were now carrying him, because he had fallen asleep. Even in his sleep, tears rolled down his face and he winced a lot.

Artemis told us we were about halfway to her house, but Rinay and I just wanted to get there so we could put Scott down. We passed a small trickle of a river and filled up four of Artemis's water bottles for all of us, because we were starting to get parched. Then we carried on with our journey through the land. On one of the paths that I assumed Artemis made, I saw the biggest willow tree I had ever seen. I knew that once we got settled into this new land, I would be back there climbing it.

We had been walking for about forty-five minutes and my legs were weakening by the minute. Scott's weight was not helping. At last we reached our destination, Artemis's house. Once we got inside, Rinay and I set Scott down on the red couch, then fell to our knees. Our legs were so tired, they collapsed.

"Why don't you guys sleep and I will prepare a room for you to stay in for the time being," said Artemis.

While we were asleep, Artemis walked past the maple wood coffee table, the yellow desk with a beautiful glass lamp, plus a lot of other things, and into the kitchen to start the dinner meal. Artemis put on a stew filled with lots of vegetables and chicken that she had caught on the other side of the island where an old guy lives. The only reason I knew this is because the rattling of pots and pans woke me up.

I stood up to check on our brother who was in pain; he looked pale and tired. I unwrapped his hand, and screamed at what I saw. His hand was pure black except for the very tips of his fingers, and his hand had a hole in his palm with lots of blood around it. Artemis came over to me and comforted me.

"I will travel to the other side of the island where my grandfather lives, and bring him back here to fix up Scott's hand," Artemis said.

"That would be really nice of you, Artemis. You don't know how much it would mean to Rinay and me if you did that," I said.

"You are very welcome, Leon. Besides it was my fault he got hurt, and I should do something about it," Artemis said.

ELLA ASHFORD

Excerpt from Descendants of the Gods

It is three days before my eleventh birthday. I am so excited. I can't focus on my homework assignment. I try to, because after this class, there is a special program about Greek mythology at the library. I look at the clock on the wall and groan. Ten more minutes to go before the class lets out.

"Helena, you're usually so focused," says my math teacher, Mr. Brush. He is grinning mischievously. He knows I am excited about Greek mythology. Unlike most of my teachers, Mr. Brush is young and vibrant and gets all his students stoked about math. He is my favorite teacher.

At that moment, the bell rings.

"Bye, Mr. Brush," I say, as I rush out the door. I run all the way to the library. I am the only person there.

"Hello," says a middle-aged man. "Looks like

you're my only student," he says, glumly.

• • •

An hour later, I walk out of the library. When I get home, I walk into the forest behind our house. It is the place I can always truly think. I think about the class. I know all the stories, but I always love to hear them over again. I have always loved Greek mythology. Sometimes I wish I could be a demigod: half-god, half-mortal. Most heroes in Greek mythology are demigods or half-bloods. But I am just a normal girl. I want a life of adventure and excitement, like in the books.

• • •

The next two days go by in a flash. Each day I return to the woods after school. I keep a pair of moccasins and a bow in a hollow log. I made the bow out of wood in the forest, so it isn't really good. I don't have any arrows, though. I would need a knife for that. A knife is what I really want for my birthday.

Finally it's the big day: my birthday, May eighteenth! The guests will be here any minute. I run around making last-minute changes. *Ring! Ring!* I hear the doorbell, and rush to the door. Family and friends are standing on the front porch. As soon as they see me, they say, "HAPPY BIRTHDAY, HELENA!" Guests stream in. The last to come in is my Aunt Matilda. She is my favorite aunt.

"How are you doing?" I ask.

"Just fine, precious, just fine," she says with an evil smile. I look up into her usually blue eyes to see that they have turned an unusual shade of red. Something's wrong.

I go to greet the other guests and, slowly, I forget about my aunt. The guests sing "Happy Birthday" and I get the first slice of cake. Finally, it's time to open the presents!

I go through one after another, reading cards, and thanking the people who gave them to me. I get lots of clothes and a few Greek mythology books, but no knife. I swallow hard, and make it to the last present. It is from my mom. I undo the wrapper slowly and see a box with a picture on it. I almost yell with triumph: it's a pocketknife! I run up to my mom and hug her.

"Thanks, Mom," I say.

"We've been together eight years now. You are old enough," she says, and gives me one more hug, then walks away to go tend to the guests.

I think about my real parents. They died eight years ago in a car accident. That is what the police said anyway. But I never really believed them. When they found the car, there were no bodies in it.

I snap out of my thoughts and see that the guests and my mother have gone out to the front porch.

"My party is over too soon," I whine to myself. I turn to get my sweater and find myself face to face with my Aunt Matilda.

"Don't worry, precious, I'll make this fast," she

hisses before I can reply. Her skin starts melting off, her face gets narrower and the leather jacket she is wearing morphs into wings. She looks like a human-sized bat with big, sharp, ugly claws. I gaze, transfixed in disbelief. Then it dawns on me: she is a fury.

I have read a lot of Greek mythology books and know almost every Greek thing by sight. I instinctively pull out my new pocketknife that till now has been snugly resting in my coat pocket.

"Stay away," I say, weakly.

The joy of my birthday party is a hazy memory. A wave of fear washes over me. What am I doing here? I should be hiding! But I have a feeling if I turn even for one second, she will… I can't even finish the thought. The fury dives for me, talons outstretched, ready to tear me apart!

ODETTE JENNINGS

Miss Delilah

The house was quiet in the middle of the night, so quiet she could hear the creaking of the floorboards as she crept down the staircase. Though the stairs were winding and irregular, she had no trouble navigating down them in the dark. People often complained about the stairs and would never attempt to use them in the dark, but habit guided her safely down. She swung around on the banister and winced as it creaked its disapproval.

In the living room the fireplace sprang to life, but she didn't even flinch. Sometimes, when she was younger, she would stare into it and wait for the wood to burn, but it never did. Every time they would turn it on, that log burned, but never turned to ash. Then her parents told her the fireplace was electric.

Some nights she would wake up and not be able to fall back asleep. Most nights, actually. Her parents thought she was sick, but the doctors reassured them it was nothing. She liked the time she had in the night, especially when it was stormy outside and she could hear the wind whistling through the trees. It was comforting, in a way, knowing she was safe inside, but it was also scary. When there was thunder and lightning she preferred to stay in bed, just in case.

Her spot by the window in the living room was illuminated by the shine of the moon. Beside the couch was a chest. On top of it were a small box, a lamp, a framed family portrait, and a vase with drooped, colorless lilies that were given to her as a present.

"Look at these beautiful flowers, darling! And they're for you!" her mom had said when they had arrived a few days ago.

"Mm-hm," she had replied, with little enthusiasm.

Her mom kept a smile on her face, and put the flowers down on the counter.

"Why don't you trim them and put them in a vase, darling?" she had scoffed at her mother, and when her mother wasn't looking, she dumped the lilies in the sink.

Now they were back on the table. And they were dead. Flowers didn't die in my house, she thought.

She sat down in her spot by the window and stared blankly at the big starry sky.

• • •

When the stars weren't out, I wondered whether my midnight walk was necessary. With no stars to gaze at, it wasn't worth wasting the sleep.

My house was rarely noticed. It wasn't the house itself; in fact, it was quite charming: lime-green exterior with perfect white trim, a beautiful garden, and a white picket fence. It was much like the other houses on the block, except for one. Unlike the rest, this house was painted a vibrant yellow with bright green trim and a red door. People would drive by and roll down their windows and point. It was practically a tourist destination. The only strange thing was, the house had only one window. At first I thought it had somehow been an oversight, but decided they must have wanted it that way.

I would have assumed the house to be empty, except for when I would see someone in that window. There was a young girl who lived inside with a slight, dainty face and distant eyes the color of soot. Her hair was like none I had ever seen, full and thick with tight curls that wound around the edges of her face. She wore the same white nightgown every time she sat in the window, but it always looked a pristine white, as if it had never been worn.

I took a deep breath as I walked past the house. One might say it was like walking by a graveyard, and in a way it was. I felt a shiver down my spine and let out a heavy breath when I reached my gate. It creaked as I slid it open, and I cursed under my breath. I didn't know what would happen to me if my parents discovered that I had gone out.

Inside, all the lights were off and I had to hold my arms out in front of me to avoid a collision. I turned the knob on my bedroom door slowly and crept inside.

My mother's face was stern the next morning. I had to get up myself instead of being dragged out of bed and to the table for breakfast. Something was up. My mother did not ask how I slept or share any neighborhood gossip. She didn't even say goodbye, or remind me not to forget my lunch when I left. I forgot it. When I called her from school, she didn't pick up the phone.

Someone poked me in the ribs, and I screamed.

"Why do you always scream like that?" my best friend, Iris, laughed. "It's as if I had broken your arm or something!"

She waved her hands in front of my face to get me out of my trance. "Hello?" she urged, "Wake up! I'm speaking!"

"I'm here. I'm just tired or something," I replied.

"Were you even listening to me?"

I nodded.

"What did I just say?" She crossed her arms and shifted her weight onto one leg, looking sassy.

"'Why are you screaming?'" I said, doing my best imitation of her. "'I didn't break your arm!' Then you waved your hands in my face and told me to wake up." I crossed my arms.

"You didn't hear me say that that creepy girl from your street was out yesterday at her mailbox, and on her way back up the steps she dropped this envelope!"

"I'm pretty sure you didn't say that," I laughed under my breath.

"See? You weren't listening!" She pulled a

mangled envelope out of her back pocket.

"Look! It's addressed to her! Let's read it!"

I snatched it out of her hand.

"Later."

She put her hands up defensively, mouthed, *Okay*, and disappeared down the hall.

My stomach growled as I walked home that afternoon. The day was warm, but the wind was picking up and blowing my hair in my face. I was glad when I reached my front door. I rushed to the kitchen, letting my backpack drop to the floor along the way. When I heard a knock, I went to the front door to let Iris in. She began talking before I opened the door.

"I've been thinking and I don't know if we should read this letter. I mean, it's not ours, and what if it says something scary or something weird and we feel bad and—"

"You're the one who took it," I pointed out.

"What if she notices it's missing?" She widened her eyes at me.

I took the letter from her hands. The name was inscribed daintily in elaborate calligraphy, with swoops and curls and flourishes. Oh, how I longed to have such beautiful handwriting. The envelope was addressed to "Miss Delilah."

"Come with me," I said.

We ran to the fence that marked the edge of my yard, which you had to stand on your tiptoes to see over. I felt the envelope crinkle in my hand and loosened my grip. On the other side of the fence the grass was cleanly cut. Flowers thrived in small pots and little patches along the pathway to the front door. Potted plants were arranged carefully on the front porch with not a single flower drooping or without vibrant color. Yet it was fall. Our yard was littered with fallen golden leaves. The flowers that bloomed in spring were gone, and the grass was no longer a bright green.

A vase of lilies sat in their window, drooped and lifeless, the ones we had given them months ago.

Iris nudged my shoulder. Her expression read *impatient*. I walked back to my front steps and sat down again. Iris followed.

"It just doesn't make sense," I muttered.

"What doesn't?"

"The flowers. The empty house. The letter."

"The flowers?"

"It's fall, Iris. Flowers don't bloom in the fall. Every house but theirs has a yard full of fallen leaves and dried up grass. I don't get it."

"Stop obsessing over it. Maybe they're special imported flowers that bloom in the fall. Maybe the house *isn't* empty. You just don't happen to be looking when the people go in and out. And people receive letters like this all the time."

I walked up to my front door and turned the door knob. The door opened and inside on the floor was an envelope. I picked it up, tentatively. Written on the front was my name, Daisy. I fumbled with the opening, pulled out the browned paper folded into thirds, and read it:

I know you have my letter.

Isaac
Steiner

ISAAC STEIMLE

Excerpt from The Kingdom of Exiles

Shen continued down the tunnel, feeling along the walls. The sounds of guards hurrying around the castle had long since faded. They had discovered the body of the soldier he had knocked unconscious, so they knew he was somewhere near. But they couldn't figure out where. He had simply melted away into the wall.

Shen sensed someone in the tunnel with him, and jumped back in surprise. But he soon made out the vague shape of his master.

"Shen. It is good to see you. I know myself that the deed is done. You have performed well," he said.

"I am honored to have served you," Shen replied.

His master sighed. "I suppose so. But you weren't so undetectable on your way out of the castle.

They found the guard you knocked out. And trust me, that damned magician has ways of finding out who did such a thing."

Shen felt his pulse accelerating. He didn't like the way this conversation was going.

"You can deal with that," he said. "The job is done. I did what you asked, for the price we agreed on."

"I don't know. The price is quite a heavy one, considering all things. It may have to change."

"I can't go much lower than what we agreed on."

"Oh, I think you can." His master sounded menacing. Shen took a small step back, and his spine brushed up against the cold, damp stone of the tunnel. He was like a cornered animal.

"The price can go down, but I still get all the other stuff you promised me." His master paused.

"All right, the other agreements still stand. But first, tell me something. Did anyone recognize you on your way out of the castle?"

"No master," Shen said. "No one but two guards." He could vaguely make out a twisted smile on the man's face.

"Good. Then no one will realize you're gone."

Shen heard the rasp of steel echo as a dagger was drawn in the tunnel. With the instincts of a veteran street fighter, Shen sprang away from the dagger as the man lunged at him. He wasn't quick enough. The cold bite of metal pierced through his jerkin and twisted inside his gut. With a roar of pain, he yanked it out by the blade, slicing his hands. Before the other man could prepare another strike, Shen turned and ran, footsteps echoing on the ground. He was almost to the door when a voice rang out behind him, sweet and thick with persuasion: "Shen, stop running. Do not go through that door."

Shen turned hesitantly. The voice was enticing, alluring; he wanted to do anything for that voice. It was a voice of pure reason and logic, a voice that could never say anything wrong. Yet a part of him thought of the danger that had befallen him moments before and told him to run.

"Listen to me, Shen," the voice called out again, coming closer. "Everything is going to be all right. Just stay where you are."

Shen was frozen, like a mouse caught in the hypnotic stare of a snake. In the dim light he caught the flash of a dagger. It came closer, but he remained still. The small voice inside his head was screaming at him to get away, but he drowned it out. *The voice says everything will be all right,* he thought. *The voice is never wrong. Just stay where you are.*

A dark figure slowly took shape in front of him, growing as it came nearer. Blood dripped from the still red dagger and hit the ground with a plop. The figure was only a foot away now. Fluidly, he raised the dagger up, and Shen stared at him, enraptured. Then the blade came flashing down and the spell broke. Shen leapt out of the way at the last moment. A whoosh of air whistled past his face as the dagger flashed by. The man's howl of rage echoed in the narrow tunnel as Shen fled, holding his blood-soaked side as he ran back for the door. He pounded on it with both fists, and the lock clicked and slid aside. As he pushed a tapestry away and stumbled out into the corridor, a flood of light suddenly attacked his eyes. He stood gasping for a moment, shielding his face. When his vision finally adjusted, he found himself staring at a group of four startled guards.

It took the guards, who had just seen a servant with blood splattered on his shirt, longer to react than Shen. He rushed at the first one with his shoulder, slamming him full force in the groin and sending him crumpled to the floor. A punch to the windpipe took out the second guard, but as soon as he was getting ready to sprint away, a guard stepped out in front of him. A sword pommel swung down towards his head. He tried to dodge the blow, but to no avail. Then everything went black.

• • •

The master watched the scene from a small,

crumbling crack in the wall to the left of the tunnel. He didn't flinch when the guard brought the heavy counterweight down on Shen's head with a sick crunching sound; it was of little consequence to him whether the boy was injured or not. His purpose had already been served. It hadn't taken much power for the boy to be convinced to poison the king. And he had done so successfully. The fact that he had escaped was troubling, though. The master preferred killing people off once they had ceased to be useful to him. Death was so much more efficient. Not to mention he enjoyed it as well, seeing the look of betrayal in his servants' eyes as they realized their beloved master no longer needed them. It was the last look they would ever have, before their faces were frozen into the grimace of death.

The master turned and glided silently down the tunnel. He needed to re-adjust his plan. It confounded him that the boy had managed to escape, but there were more important things for him to think about. One of them, now that the king was dying, was how to kill the two princes.

• • •

Captain Rogan was in his office, listening to the latest report by one of his soldiers. He scratched his graying beard in exasperation. By now, he was getting frustrated with the hunt for the assassin. Patience was not his strong suit. And worse, the king was taking the effects of the poison. The physician said that he only had a few hours more at best. It made the search all the more important.

"The guard we found has recovered from his head injury, sir," the patrolman said. Like all the guards, he wore a green and blue tunic, the colors of the Keldorian flag, over a chainmail shirt. "Unfortunately, he can only give a vague description of the man who attacked him. And he doesn't know where the assassin went, either. We've searched the castle all over, sir, and there is no way he could have gotten out."

"He can't have just disappeared into thin air!" Rogan said, irritated.

"I don't know where he is, but there are too many places to hide in this castle. He could be anywhere."

"Check all the halls, rooms and passageways. Search everyone's living quarters, even if they protest. Tear the castle apart stone by stone if you need to. I want the assassin found!" The captain almost roared the words.

The patrolman nodded and left the room in a hurry. The door swung back open a few seconds later, though, and the patrolman stepped timidly back inside.

"What is it now?" Rogan asked, massaging his temples.

"Sir, a watchman is here to see you. He claims it's about the assassin."

Abruptly, the captain stood up, pushing back his chair. "Send him in," he ordered.

Nodding, the patrolman backed out of the door,

and a short moment later the watchman stumbled through, heaving breathlessly. "Captain, we caught the assassin in one of the servant's corridors. The rest of us are still waiting there. No one else knows yet."

"Quick, we must tell the prince. This is great news. There is still hope for the king." said Rogan.

The guard nodded, and then replied, "At once, sir, but there is one more thing you need to know. We think that the assassin is—"

His words were cut short by the door exploding open, slamming with a crack into his back and knocking him down. On top of him fell the body of the patrolman, a knife buried in his neck, blood spurting from it in a constant stream. Three men entered swiftly, holding keen steel swords coated in crimson, and garbed in black cloaks draped over dark armor, and masks. One leaned down and dispatched the fallen guard with a quick stab to the back. It all happened in a matter of seconds.

Rogan's sword was drawn instantly, ready to fight his way out, despite the odds. Then two more men armed with crossbows stepped through the door, aiming their deadly weapons at Rogan's heart.

"Drop your weapon if you wish to live," one of the black-clad soldiers said in a harsh voice.

Knowing he was hopelessly outnumbered, Rogan reluctantly dropped his sword. Rage flowed through his veins like wildfire at the thought that these traitorous dogs had killed his guards and come to threaten him.

"Who are you? What are you doing here?" he demanded.

Soundlessly, two of the men came forward. Shoving him down onto his desk, they bound his hand behind his back with strong rope. It cut into his skin.

"You will come with us," one of them said, in a flat, unemotional voice. "You will answer for your crimes in front of the masterful one. It is he who will decide your fate, as well as the fates of the so-called 'princes.'"

Chills crept up the captain's spine. The

poisoning of the king was part of a much greater conspiracy, one he had failed to protect the royal family from. With despair, he realized that if what these men said was true, everything was lost.

RUEVEAR
Dream School

My dream school would be huge. It would be a boarding school, but not a dreadful one, like others; it would be fabulous.

In the school's main building, there would be many floors, and on each floor there would be a flying glass elevator to go to different rooms throughout the building. The classrooms would be miraculous, because of the teachers and the assignments. The students would pick their classes; whatever they wanted to learn about was taught. Students would also be able to choose how long they wanted to take classes (anywhere from five minutes to all day) and when they wanted the class in their schedule. The teachers would be very nice and fun. Basically they would be there only to make sure everyone was safe and being nice to each other. The students would come up with the assignments, and there would be no homework or tests unless the students wanted them.

The gym would be a separate building with many areas where many activities take place. It would have big swimming pools and hot tubs, volleyball and basketball courts, an indoor soccer field with real grass, and a climbing wall on each wall of the gym.

The cafeteria would have buttons that you press to order anything you wanted, and it would pop out of the wall under the button on gold trays in a matter of seconds. The floors of the cafeteria would be aqua-blue marble. Seats would be red velvet easy chairs with wheels and gold embellishments. The tables would be made of clear glass with colorful suns and moons painted on them. Everyone could chose where they sat and who they wanted to sit by; if someone wanted to sit by the president, for instance, the principal would make sure he came.

The bathrooms at the school would have pine-green toilets and purple stalls; the stalls would be like little rooms. The sinks would be made of pine-green marble, the soap would be handcrafted by artists from around the world, even Leonardo da Vinci, and the towels would be purple with embroidered names on them of all the students attending at the time.

The library would be the size of thirteen football fields put together. The room would be one of the most amazing parts of the school; every book imaginable would be there, even the classified books from government agencies. Laptop and desktop computers would be located at maple-wood desks with comfy blue desk chairs to sit in throughout the library. Each shelf in the library would be over forty feet high; gold sliding ladders would be attached by the top of the shelves for getting books from unreachable heights. Everything to keep you comfortable would be in there. People could stay all day, every day in the library.

The hallways at the school would have red marble floors, purple shimmery walls with gold swirly trim, and different chandeliers every ten feet. Some of the chandeliers were made of colored glass, and others were made of metal and cloth with animals and plants decorating them. On the walls would be real, famous paintings, like the Mona Lisa, Picassos, and other magnificent paintings by famous and unheard-of artists.

Every room in the buildings would have a different door, with a different story; no door was the same. Some of the stories on the doors would be: an orange door with painted blue birds at the top that came from a family of thirteen on Madagascar, and others would come from companies in China.

The dorms would be tree houses in oak, maple, and cedar trees outside the main building. Each tree house would be a different color. No one would have to share rooms and everyone would be allowed to choose everything that goes in their room. They would be allowed to have anything they wanted in there. If someone wanted to rearrange their room, there would be magic buttons to press for changing the furniture, floor, walls, and decorations.

Each person attending the school would be

given a pet, real or mythological. Students would be allowed to carry their animals around during school or have a teacher look after them in their dorms. For instance, you could have a purple orangutan, a Great Dane, or a unicorn. Each person also would be given an iPod Touch, Nano, Classic, or Shuffle, an iPhone, MacBook Pro or Air laptop, an iMac, or an iPad Classic or Mini, but they also could choose to have all of them, as long as they were from the Apple company.

In a separate building from the main building, connected by a yellow brick pathway, would be a mall-like place. In the building would be all the stores that people wanted to have, except food stores. Not a single student had to pay for anything. Everything was free, and in endless supply. This building would have many floors and spiral staircases.

Parents could visit whenever they liked; the school would even pay for plane tickets or gas and a place to stay. If a student wished to travel somewhere, like London, England, the school would pay for all the expenses. They would send a teacher to go along with the student for safety and company.

It would be free for the students and families to go to the school, except for a fifty dollar fee, but that would be it. There would be no uniforms; all the students' clothing would be purchased from the mall-like building.

The school's mascot would be a yellow-and-orange striped flying kangaroo (the principal's favorite animal and pet).

The outside area around the school would be filled with beautiful flowers, berries, fruit trees, vegetable gardens, pathways, fountains, trampolines, tire swings, slides, jungle gyms, and other fun and beautiful objects.

No chores or consequences would be given to the students. They would be able to meet any celebrity they wanted, dead or alive, fake like the Mad Hatter, or real like Walt Disney, whenever they wanted to.

Each student would be delivered to the school

by a blue and silver train. The school would own submarines, boats, helicopters, trains, planes, and automobiles for students and teachers, for exploration. Each student attending the school would own a limo of any color and type. All students would also have a private doctor of their choice to keep them healthy and happy.

Usually, students who attend the school live to be at least one hundred and twenty-five years old, and have been known to live as many as two hundred years.

A magic shield and dragons would protect the school from harm. The school would be located in Ireland, and would be a magical, amazing, and spectacular school to attend; most people would stay at the school their whole lives.

Robyn
Reimnitz

KORBYN REIMNITZ

Excerpt from an as-yet-untitled novel

The full moon shone brightly on Scarmoor Forest. The air was crisp and fresh and a gentle breeze rustled the needles in the trees that stood tall above the forest floor. A dirt path wound its way through the thick bushes, twisting and turning like a great serpent. It was also slowly being overgrown by the giant ferns and chokecherry bushes that fenced the path, for it had been over a year since anyone had trod upon it. But this path was no ordinary trail that led to a town or village, this was a path that led to freedom. This was the path to the Great Portal.

Although it was over a mile away, the Great Portal's pale green glow was visible. It was a great beacon of hope. It was a beacon that showed there was a way to escape from this terrible land. If one would journey through the Great Portal, they would come upon a panorama free of dark magic, cruelty, and creatures of the shadow; land free from the slaught-stitchers, the horrible man-made monsters that carried out orders so cruel and terrible that not even the most cunning, battle-hardened warrior would dare to interfere with their unthinking missions. The abominations would not distinguish between killing a soldier in battle and a defenseless mother and infant, weeping at their feet for mercy. Once, good souls of the many an unfortunate victim had been unable to resist the will of darkness as the very faces of evil grinned and placed them in monstrous bodies—rotting flesh and coarse thread taking the place of skin and living sinew—and were forced to murder and pillage. A perpetual life of uncontrollable slaughter and misery; that was the fate that loomed after death on the wrong side of the Portal.

A slight rustle in the dense bushes of Scarmoor was picked up by a pair of long, pointed ears, the ears of a tall, thin, elven lady, seated astride a white horse. She rode in complete silence, making no more sound than a fox stalking a hare at twilight. At her side she carried a slender, elven sword, its elegant blade marked with ancient runes. Four more horses followed her, each with an elven warrior seated on its back. They were equally quiet and carried swords and fighting knives on their belts and sashes. The shoeless horses seemed to be trained in the art of stealth, for their hooves nimbly evaded all obstacles that littered their path, sidestepping fallen branches and twigs while their eyes remained trained ahead. Another rustle from the bushes drew the five travelers to a halt. The elven lady's ears twitched as the rustling grew louder. They climbed from their mounts and drew their weapons, still making no more sound than a speck of dust falling on a feather bed.

Suddenly, an indescribable sensation pierced through the minds of the horses and the warrior elves, sending them into a writhing fit of pain. Agony seemed to course through the very passages of their brains. It felt as though a spike of excruciating pain was trying to breach the walls of their minds and penetrate their inner thoughts. The elven lady tried to aid her screaming comrades, she herself seemed unaffected by the icy wave of cutting pain. One, then two of the five horses succumbed to the anonymous pain, and fell lifeless to the ground. The remaining three stumbled, whinnying and screeching, attempting to make a desperate run, battling for control over their writhing bodies against the unseen torture. Finally, after what seemed an eternity in Hell, the pain subsided. The elves collapsed to the ground, utterly exhausted. The horses, finally freed from the waves of mental agony, and in a mad panic, bolted into the night, abandoning their riders in the face of an unknown threat.

Out of the bushes stepped a tall, black figure. It looked like no more than a silhouette, its dark form almost ghostly, save for its face. On its head, which blended into its shadowed body, was a gleaming silver actor's mask. A sadistic smile cut across it like a gaping wound, topped with small eyes, identical in shape to the mouth, but much smaller and inverted. It was a blinding silver that shone brighter than the light of the moon, casting an eerie glow over the scene.

From their humbled position, the warriors looked to their leader for any sign of a plan. Their dark panic, however, was only mirrored in the eyes of the lady. As the elves looked on with a feeling of dismay, a screeching magpie flew down out of the night sky and perched on the dark figure's shoulder. Its feathers were jet black with patches of the same brilliant silver of its ghostly master's mask. From behind the sadistic figure stepped six hideous creatures. The elves cringed in disgust at the sight of the disfigured monsters. Two of them had an extra arm sewn onto them, and one had the small head of a monkey attached to its side. The seams that held the creatures together were made of thick string and no eyes were in the black sockets that filled the emptiness above their decaying noses. The shadowy figure emitted three sharp shrieks of mind-numbing commands that threatened to send the elves back into the horrific state they had just recovered from. The vicious mental torture seemed to be a way for the dark creatures to communicate. The zombie-like minions grunted in return and seemed to understand the piercing sounds that had just emerged from their commander's shadowy mind. They pulled wicked-looking weapons from their belts and advanced on the elves. Rusted blades with serrated edges threatened gory, inflicted wounds in the elves' pale flesh.

One of the elves rushed forward with a fearsome war cry. He clashed swords with a three-armed creature, and the two of them became locked in mortal combat. The other elves ran to assist their comrade and slashed at their abhorrent opponents with speed that a human could never muster. The elves fought bravely, but soon found that these murderous warriors were not average opponents by any stretch of the imagination. These vile creatures did not attempt to block the elves' swift blows; they allowed the razor-like steel to slice their rotting flesh, and even sever their limbs. Again and again the sleek blades sliced the monsters' rough skin, but the beasts appeared to be unharmed and continued to drive the elves back. One, two, three, then four of the elves fell prey to their opponents' bloodied blades until only the lady elf was left alive.

Blood dripping from both her shoulder and thigh, she realized she could not hope to win this fight with strength. Narrowing her eyes and taking a deep breath, she whispered a strange phrase in an enchanting foreign language. A bolt of blinding light shot from her hand, puncturing the body of one of the hideous creatures. It fell to the ground with a loud grunt, blood streaming from the enormous hole in its muscled chest. A green light the color of the Portal emerged from where the monster's heart should have been and ascended up towards the night sky.

"May the spirits be with you," whispered the elf to the mesmerizing light.

The pale green ethereal form ascended out of sight as the elf turned back towards the enemy. Her wounds were draining her strength, both physically and mentally, with every pump of her heart making it life-threatening for her to exert herself with arcane defenses for a second time. She needed time to heal. She was losing blood too fast. She had to make it to the Portal. Extra time and kindhearted peasants with plentiful larders and medical aid awaited her on the other side. Her best bet was simply to run.

Blood streamed from her leg, dyeing her white cloak red, but her peerless endurance gave her a fighting chance in the realm of speed. A fighting chance was the best she could hope for. Soon she was breathing heavily, and sweat was dripping from her brow. Her pace slowed. The monsters' pace, however, quickened, if anything. The masked master's magpie soared and dived above the elf's head, screeching wildly. As the elf ran, the Great Portal came closer in view, but the chances of her making the next quarter mile grew smaller. She looked back with vision blurred by pain, and saw her pursuers steadily gaining on her.

"I have to make it," whispered the elf between

breaths. "The price of my failure is too great for this world to afford."

SAM HERON

Excerpt from Surfaced

All I remembered was cold. Cold, darkness, and utter pain. Nothing more, nothing less. But then...*then*...there was the faintest trace of light, something gorgeous in its simplicity. I had no idea what it was, but it was comforting under the spider web of agony. I recognized the affliction soon enough; it could only be explained as something exploding inside of me, not being able to breathe, my lungs aching. And then, I surfaced.

I saw that the speckles of light came from the stars, the beautiful golden-silver flickers looking disjointed yet complementary to the blackish blue sky. The deflating raft rocked as it hit the sand bank. The sudden jerk awoke me from my pitiful, agonizing feeling. As soon as I realized that land was near, hope and joy filled my body. I cast a long, hopeful gaze at the island. I could only imagine its sweet soft sand.

The land suddenly felt like a goal I had finally reached.

"Finally!" I yelped. Anguish swept through my body. I screamed. My weak arms lifted my dehydrated body into a sitting position. My body was cold, for the salty water still covered me. My old college sweatshirt, wrapped around where my leg should be, was dripping with scarlet blood. Such a revolting sight. My flesh was still exposed, as the bloodstained sweatshirt wasn't big enough.

I cleansed the wound as best I could with my socks, even though they were already drenched with the salty water. It was like getting a bunch of paper cuts and diving into a pool of lemon juice.

Once I cleansed my wound, I made the dangerous attempt to dog paddle to the little mound of land in the distance. The only things keeping me from using the raft to get to the island was that it had no oars and was stuck behind the sandbank.

My weak leg kicked fiercely at the icy water. A wave of drowsiness crashed through me. My arms felt heavy. Anger filled my veins, giving me a sudden surge of strength. The land seemed to be on the edge of the horizon, yet, soon enough, my one good foot touched the soft, elegant sand. It glided between my toes. The blue-black sky was hit with orange rays of light, making the dark sky into a purplish pink. It was beautiful.

I crawled onto the beach. The front of my body was covered in sand, which irritated my skin. I shivered as I reached the warm, dry sand. I hadn't felt warmth in what seemed like weeks. I was always cold, always drenched in the icy water. I lay there for hours, absorbing the heat. I eventually drifted off into a deep slumber.

• • •

"Evacuate! There are three rafts left!" the captain shouted.

"But, sir, there are still roughly a hundred passengers on board!" a sailor added.

"Stuff 'em in the rafts! Put in as many people as you can!" the captain said, brushing us towards the remaining rafts.

People's faces turned pale, their bodies sank; it seemed as if they had already died inside. The bomb exploding on the rear end of the boat reflected in their eyes. I barely escaped having a flying piece of wood jab its way through my skull. I shuffled towards one of the rafts. Four people already sat in it, snuggled together with expressionless, shocked faces. I should have noticed the ropes were thin. I would have had more time to get more people aboard before the rope gave out. I hate myself right now.

Before I could react, the ropes snapped and I ended up free-falling. I looked up at the tilted boat. People screamed, but I couldn't hear them. The shock of falling somehow temporarily deafened me. The raft slapped onto the water, letting everyone bounce onto the rubber surface. But I wasn't that lucky. I bounced off the side and splashed into the icy water. I was so shocked and scared that I didn't move. People *stretched out their arms trying to grasp my hand.*

"Come on, sweetheart, I got you!" a man shouted, as he maneuvered his body out more to reach me. I didn't reach back. The blue fin popped out of the greenish water. I should have expected it, for we were on a shark watch. It was a part of the three-month cruise we were on.

Three people were reaching for me; the shark was approaching quickly, but I just lay floating on the water.

• • •

Then I awoke. My head ached.

"What the hell?" I said, annoyed. This had been a very detailed, strange dream. My leg—well, the wound where my leg *was*—ached. I realized how hungry I was. I knew it would be difficult catching food, considering my being one-legged. I retied the sweatshirt onto my stump. I tried several times to stand and balance on one leg, but it just didn't work.

My energy had disappeared at that point.

Once half an hour had passed, I crawled up and down the beach searching for a long stick to support my weight—a crutch. I kept throwing the useless sticks behind me. My anger and frustration grew more and more as the moments passed. My eyes glanced across the landscape. A staff with great potential finally came in my sight. I grasped it and felt the texture of the staff. It was smooth. I crawled around with the staff trying to find a sharp rock. I saw a very sharp, pointy rock.

"Perfect," I said to myself. I sawed my way through the staff to make it the right height. My arm ached after the constant movement and firm grasp on the rock. Towards the top of the staff, it split off and grew two more branches. It would be perfectly fit under my arm. The branches were too long, of course, so I had to cut them both down quite a bit. I had made a crutch for myself.

I propped myself up and slipped it under my thin, weak arm. It worked, though it wasn't all that comfortable. It needed padding. I stumbled along on the edge of the forest, grabbing leaves and vines, then out of the greenery and back to the beach. I sat upon a grand blue-grey rock. It overlooked the beautiful bright blue sea. The waves danced and floated across the water until they finally crashed onto the soft sand. Every once in a while, I would see a fin appear. I'm pretty sure they were just dolphins, but they reminded me of the fin that approached me in my dream. I don't know why I dreamed that. I mean, I'm from Oklahoma. I rarely think of the ocean or sharks.

I stacked the leaves gently where my arm would rest and tied them down securely with a vine. I tested it out once again trying to adjust to the padding. It was quite comfortable. It actually made me move more quickly.

"Aren't I clever?" I congratulated myself.

My stomach was growling at this point. I tumbled along the shore searching for food. No luck. I didn't want to go too far into the forest, but that was where meat was. I shoved my way through vines, bushes, and trees searching for a bird at least. I studied the trees, barely blinking. I flutter of feathers brushed passed me. The bird perched on a twig sticking out of the ground. It was a beautiful bird, I had to admit. I hated killing animals, but it was just something I had to do in order to survive. The bird chirped sweetly. Colorful feathers decorated its body. I had to stop thinking about it and just kill the damn thing. I looked at my surroundings trying to find something that could kill the bird easily. A ridged rock lay just in front of it.

I slowly reached out to the ridged rock. I did so as quietly as possible so as not to startle my precious meal. I made sure I had a firm grasp and perfect aim before I launched it. It soared through the air. Just before the rock pierced the bird's thin neck, the bird cocked its head and noticed the inanimate object flying towards it. It cawed, then choked up blood from its neck. It was nasty, but worth it. The rock was still stuck in the neck.

I collected driftwood from the sandy shore and

put it in a neat pile. I skinned the bird and stuck a stick into the rear end and out the front end. After the constant rubbing back and forth of two sticks to start a fire, my hands ached and became stiff. Sparks collected onto the driftwood and were set afire. I smiled as the hard work paid off. I roasted the bird for at least an hour until it was finally cooked. My first bite was small. I had never tasted bird before, since I'm a vegetarian, so I had to check it out. It tasted...pretty good. It was surprising. I finished off the bird, feeling satisfied. I lay there for a bit resting my stomach. I needed to find a water source tomorrow or I'd be dead in a few days. As the tiny fire grew into a beach bonfire, it provided wonderful warmth to me. I dozed off into a restful slumber. My dream continued...

• • •

People shouted at me; as the shark drew closer, the shouts grew louder. I froze. At this point there was no time to save myself. I accepted that I would probably not survive this time. The shark breached and dove at my leg. Its many sharp teeth sliced its way through my flesh and bone and swam away, satisfied. The water around me slowly turned scarlet. I turned to face the three terrified passengers, but before I could, somebody had already pulled me out of the icy water. I lay in the middle of the raft oozing blood. A pool of it surrounded me. I became cold.

"It's okay honey. Just listen to me. You're gonna be fine. Now tell me: what's your name?" The man hovering over me looked concerned.

I tried to spit out the answer, but all that came out was a cough of blood. It splattered all over the man's face. A look of disgust and a little sickness appeared on his face.

"Help me take off her sweatshirt people! Hurry! We need to stop the bleeding!" he shouted frantically.

"Au- A- Aub- Aub- Aubry M- Mich- Michaels-Michaelson." I painfully responded. It was an effort talking. It felt as if I couldn't breathe, as if there was

a wall in my throat blocking the words from coming out.

• • •

I awoke, once again confused by the disturbingly detailed dream. It's weird that it continued right where it left off. It must mean something, but I just can't put my finger on it. My head throbbed. I fell back onto the sand. I looked at my wound and noticed blood pouring out. I had lost a lot of it during the night. I stuck the nub of leg I had left straight up, pointing towards the sky, forcing the blood back down. It wasn't a very comfortable position, but I have to do what I have to do to survive. I untied the sweatshirt for a few minutes, so blood wouldn't clog up. Before I could shout in frustration, I retied my sweatshirt.

"When will a ship come by?!" I shouted as loudly as I could, not expecting a response. I exhaled loudly. It was almost a sigh. I propped myself up with my crutch and headed out to look for water. The chirps of birds grew louder. It was strange. I haven't heard the birds the whole time I was here, and now they seemed oddly loud.

For the first time since I've been here, I realized I had no knowledge or remembrance of surfacing. How did I suddenly wake up on a raft, missing a leg, clueless, hungry, and thirsty? The only conclusion I could wrap my mind around was that it had something to do with my dream. I knew it was out of the ordinary, but it was the best I've got. Or maybe this was all a horrifying nightmare. I had to cling to these thoughts in order to simply remain sane. I had to keep my mind settled on something less terrifying than the fact that this could be real, that this could be my life. That I was shipwrecked and stranded on an island. That I'd be legless forever. That was not an option to think about. I know I was giving up early, but it was better to accept the fact that I might never get off this island than waste my life trying to find a passing ship.

At one point in my journey through the forest, the chirps grew louder than anything I have ever heard. The slope of going downhill had become overly steep, making me on the verge of falling. Flashes of my dreams filled my head, causing me hallucinate. My imagination was starting to meld with reality. The crashing waves from my dream poured through the actual forest in front of me. The shark swam through the trees. A wave with the raft of people on it lurched over the greenery. I was so confused and dizzy that my head ached. I crashed on the cushy mossy bed that lay beneath me. I fell asleep, but this time, didn't dream. Only blackness swam within my eyelids. Something didn't feel right.

I awoke drearily. It had most likely been about two hours, considering the position of the sun before I fell asleep and now. The sound of trickling water. I assumed it was rain. It was still night, but now stars speckled everywhere. Not a cloud in the sky. If it wasn't rain…

I quickly stood and looked in front of me, and

found a skinny stream flowing. My mouth dropped as I shoved my face in the water. The ice...cold...water. I felt it running down my throat satisfying my organs. I removed the sweatshirt from my wound and stuck my leg-nub in the water. I let the fresh water cleanse my wound on its own, while my sweatshirt was getting cleansed at the same time. The sweatshirt laid on rocks that peeked from the water as it washed the bloodstains almost completely out. I took off all of my clothes and laid them next to my sweatshirt. I washed my body free of dirt, sand, and seawater, and did the same with my hair. I put my clothes on a rock on which the sun was radiating. I found myself a nice, smooth, flat rock and set out as the sun slowly evaporated the trickling drops of water from my body. I nearly dozed off.

I quickly sat up. The sun was starting to set. I had to hurry back to the beach before dark. The dim pinkish sky had wondering, curious stars. I hopped over to the rock where my clothes had been drying. I leaned against the rock as I hopped into my shorts. I slipped into my T-shirt and stuck each arm into my sweater. I zipped it up after I securely tied the slightly damp sweatshirt around the stub. I drank a lot of water before heading back to the beach. On the way, I grabbed a couple of vines and tied it as securely as possible to keep the loss of blood low. I stumbled up the overly steep hill with my crutch. I nearly fell backwards when I reached the top. Brushing my way through the trees, my crutch left a trail in the dirt. I saw a small ray of light stretch through the thickness of vines, bushes, and trees. Eventually, I managed to break through the forest and trudge along in the sand. I came back in time to keep a lookout for passing ships. I knew it was a waste of time, but I thought I might as well try on the times when I didn't need to do anything.

Little by little, my wound's aching was fading. I looked over to the horizon as I watched the sea swallow the sun. The sea would spit it up once again in the morning. I smoothed the sand into a perfect figure to fit my shape. It formed around my silhouette comfortably. I was hoping to continue my strange dreams. For some reason, I felt safe in the dreams, as if they were the only possessions I've had since arriving here. The crashing waves came in rhythm as I tuned it into a sweet, soothing song. They rocked me to sleep, and this time, my dream did continue…

• • •

My vision blurred as I looked at where I thought my leg was. I screeched in terror and shock to find the oozing blood covering the bottom of the raft. It was a cold, wet blanket of scarlet that the others were looking at in disgust.

"You're okay, you're okay. I've got you," the man said, taking off my sweatshirt and wrapping it around my wound.

"I d-d-don't fee-feel so w-w-well," I stuttered.

"She's starting to look pale, Jon," said one of the two women. She was wrapped in a coat beside me.

"Yes, I know, Claudia. She is losing a lot of blood. I'm trying as best I can to stop it. Now, hand me the first aid kit." He pointed to the end of the raft where supposedly the first aid kit was.

Claudia tossed the kit to Jon. He scrambled through the small plastic box as he found medical tape. He wrapped it around the sweatshirt as tightly as he could. Leaning back, he sighed in relief and wiped his forehead free from any wandering sweat drops. Claudia looked somewhat relieved. The other woman looked shocked, but still tried the best she could to assist Claudia. Then...

● ● ●

I awoke in a cold sweat. I looked out at the ocean as something caught my eye. I couldn't believe it. My mind was racing with hopes and possibilities. I quickly stood and focused better on the figure. An orange raft, with someone flailing around in it, trying to paddle to shore. I couldn't tell if this was a dream

or not. I pinched myself. Nope, it was real. Damn.
When will things start to make sense?

RIVER KISLER
Excerpt from The Jason Knight Files

Jason Knight, age fifteen, was just leaving the gym. He took a martial arts class every Tuesday after school and now he was biking home down Lincoln Avenue. The sun was setting slowly. Jason glanced at the glowing surface of his watch: *6:20.* He was making good progress. By the time he got home he would be able to work on some homework before dinner.

No, he corrected himself, *I'll get home, goof off until dinner, watch a movie, and go to bed. In the morning I'll wake up early, rush to finish all my homework, wolf down my breakfast, and hurry off to school.*

Jason crested a hill, then stopped by what looked like an abandoned construction site to stretch his legs. He was about to get back on his bike when he saw a tall man in a suit clutching a briefcase and running, crouched, toward a hole in the fence surrounding the area.

That's odd, thought Jason. *What would a man like that be doing in a place like this?*

Jason biked by this construction site just about every day and had never seen anyone either enter or come out. He was curious and decided to follow the man and see what it was like in there.

Jason crept through the hole then forward through the maze of storage containers, rubbish heaps, and heavy equipment, trying to be as quiet as possible. When he got to the end of the containers, he heard the crunch of boots on gravel, and stopped abruptly at a small, cleared area, bent down behind a forklift, and peered around the corner.

Jason could only see one man, but it was not the tall one he had followed at first. This man was wearing an expensive leather jacket, cargo pants, and combat boots. He had jet black hair and tan skin and an impatient expression on his face. While Jason watched him with a mix of interest and uncertainty, the tall man in the suit appeared from around the corner. Jason hadn't noticed before, but the tall guy had a strange scar over his left eye in the shape of an arch.

When the two men were about an arm's length apart, the dark-haired man said in a gruff voice, "Do you have the photos?"

The man with the suit opened his briefcase and produced what looked like a stack of cards held together with a rubber band.

Jason watched as the tall, suited man began to hand the other guy the photographs, but, in a smooth movement, a gun appeared in the dark-haired man's hand. Jason almost cried out in surprise, the weapon was drawn so fast. The dark-haired man raised the gun, and, before the suited guy could react, fired two times. The first shot hit the suited man in the gut, throwing him backward, and the second went wide, shattering a brick and sending up sparks. Too stunned to move, Jason glanced at the man that had been shot; he was lying on the ground, his face a mask of blood.

Jason quickly looked away, then carefully turned back in time to see the dark-haired man hide the body under one of the old crates, then collect the photos and put them in the briefcase with a grim look of satisfaction.

Is this really happening to me? Jason thought, as he scrambled forward and fought a nauseous feeling.

As he turned around and began running quietly toward his bike, his foot caught on a piece of metal and he tripped, knocking over a bucket that rolled into a storage container with a loud crash. The dark-haired man looked up and saw Jason running away; he raised the gun and fired three times. The weapon was equipped with a silencer, so Jason didn't hear anything until the bullets punctured the container beside him. The dark-haired man fired again; this time the shot grazed Jason's face, and he cried out in pain and disbelief. He kept running, though he realized his cheek was bleeding. He was tiring fast and knew he was going to have to think of something—quickly.

He looked around and spotted a ladder leaning against a crate of mortar. Grabbing a brick, he grasped the ladder and began climbing. He reached the top and crouched down just as the dark-haired man rounded the corner, gun in hand. Jason stood up and dropped the brick. He had timed it perfectly. The man crumpled, the case slipping from his hands and clattering to the ground.

Jason jumped down, ready to run. Looking one last time at the knocked-out man with the gun, Jason noticed the briefcase lying at his side. Remembering the photos, and thinking that they might be crucial evidence, he quickly grabbed the briefcase and scrambled back to his bike. In his mind, the words, *I just saw someone get shot; I just knocked out the killer with a brick,* seemed almost unreal, like a dream he would wake up from any minute. But he was not dreaming.

Jason pedaled hard, urging the bike to go faster. He had already decided to go to the police first and call his mom as soon as he knew what was going on. He stopped at a busy corner and asked an elderly lady for directions to the nearest police station. She looked at him in alarm.

"You're bleeding. Are you okay, dear?"

Jason didn't know whether to tell her the truth or not, but decided he didn't have time to explain everything that had just happened to him.

"I'm okay...just need to get to the police quickly. Please tell me...which way?"

The woman pointed and gave him instructions. "Be careful, dear," she called as Jason raced off.

He had gone half a mile before he caught sight of the station. Flat and ugly, it reminded Jason of an office building and had a revolving glass door. He ran forward, sweat and blood pouring freely down his face. The receptionist at the front desk looked up in surprise. Jason grimaced, imagining what a sight he must be, dressed in his torn school shirt and his cheek a mess where the bullet had hit him.

"I need help!" he cried, the shock starting to

overcome him. "There's been a…you've got to…!"

"Calm down," said the lady. "I'm calling in an officer. He will be able to help you. Can you give me your parents' phone number?"

Jason told her his mom's number while the receptionist led him to a chair and gave him an antiseptic wipe and a Band-Aid for his cheek. A moment later the officer walked in. When he realized how scared Jason was, he sat down and gave him his attention.

The next hour was a blur. Jason remembered his mother arriving and fussing over him, then his being led into a small room with a surveillance camera. Another woman, a psychologist, came in and asked Jason questions. Later, his mother and the lady went into the adjoining room and Jason picked up snatches of conversation, like, "Jason is very mature for his age. Most other children would suffer traumatic side effects."

After the police let them go, Jason's mother bundled him into the car and took him straight to the hospital emergency room. The doctor said that Jason was in good shape and that he would recover shortly, although he was advised to skip school for a while. This would mean long, boring days at home, Jason realized, but, then again, he was relieved that he wouldn't need to rush back into the hustle and bustle of school right away.

They got home after nine o'clock and Jason was ready to collapse into bed when his mom got a call from the police saying that an expert had looked at the evidence and determined a possible threat to the White House. The Secret Service were very concerned and wanted to interview Jason at once. The officer gave directions over the phone, and Jason and his mom got ready to go. As Jason stepped into the car, he wondered what was going on and what kind of danger he'd stumbled into. His mom started the car and they drove out of the driveway towards downtown D.C.

LEMONIE
Excerpt from Life of Kai

"Just take her tonight!" I yell across the room at Talia. "I'm going to the movies with Jake. We've been planning this for months!"

"Well, I'm going to the movies with my boyfriend, Joseph."

"It's your turn."

"No, it's your turn."

"Stop it, guys." Mom walks into the kitchen. "What are you guys even fighting about?"

"Who has to take Charlie tonight!"

"Kai, it's your turn," says Mom.

"Why my turn?" I ask.

"Because...umm...you must have done something wrong that we haven't punished you for."

So, yeah, that's my mom for you. With four kids, she plays favorites and I am definitely not one of them.

Oh, sorry, I forgot to introduce myself. I am Kai Anderson, I am twelve years old, and I love—I mean *love*—video games. I have a nineteen-year-old brother named Gabe, a seventeen-year-old sister, Talia, and a younger sister, Charlie, who is two. I guess that's my life.

Let's get back to the story.

"Fine, I will take Charlie," I say.

That night I get my helmet on, my knee pads, and my elbow pads, walk into the garage, look around a bit, and—there it is, my jewel, something I could not live without. No, not video games: my skateboard.

"Now, Charlie, you are going to stand right here in the middle of the skateboard and my legs are going to be right here over your head, so don't worry. All right."

And we are off. The busy streets of New York. The wind rushing through my hair. We ride for thirty minutes. It feels like two hours. Finally I see the movie theater.

"We are going to the movies with Jake, and you are going to sit quietly while we are watching the movie," I say.

All is well and then a biker swerves in front of me. There's a mud puddle on the right and fast cars on the left. I think quickly and—*whoosh*—I take a sharp turn to the right. SPLASH!

"Oh no! Mom's going to be mad!" I yell.

All the people in the cars around me stare. I am, like, awkward. In a very high-pitched voice, Charlie laughs.

When I look at the time, it is twenty past seven. The movie started at seven. I was late and all muddy. So I carry my muddy skateboard, kneepads, elbow pads, and Charlie back home. It's farther than I thought. So I make Charlie walk half the way.

"Kai, I trusted you with her," Mom says. "I can't believe how you got her and yourself all muddy like that. Especially since we have that big banquet for your father's work tonight."

"Oh, that's tonight? I thought it was next week!

Sorry about that. I will go wash Charlie off. Give her a bath."

The only problem is that Charlie hates taking baths. When I get out of that bathroom, I look like a rag doll that has been run over by a truck a few times. I look horrible.

I run up to my room to get ready for the banquet. I get my slacks and my button-down shirt, my gray vest, and my purple-and-gray-striped tie. I look great and amazing, except for one thing: my hair. Yeah, I said it: my hair.

I get out my flat iron. I have very, very, *very* curly hair, so I have to straight-iron it. I just don't see why boys can't straight-iron their hair. It is perfectly fine. So don't judge me.

I walk downstairs when I'm finished and everyone is staring at me.

Talia says, "Wow, you clean up nice."

"Thanks," I reply.

Everyone looks amazing. Gabe is wearing a vest, suit, tie, and slacks. Dad is wearing the same thing as Gabe and me. Mom is wearing a long, dark-purple dress with a slit about halfway up. Charlie is wearing a purple flower dress about knee length with two thick shoulder straps. And Talia is wearing a purple strapless dress. It poofs out at the hip and goes down to just above the knee.

We get into the car and drive halfway across town to the banquet.

When we get there everyone is sitting at the table eating soup with their spoons. My family comes in laughing. We sit down and act about as normal as we can. Really, I don't know the difference between a soup spoon and a regular spoon. The night just gets more embarrassing. Like, I end the night by drinking out of the finger-wash bowl, like a dog. People think I *am* a dog. Which I guess I understand. And then Charlie farts.

THE AUTHORS

EZRA AGUILAR is twelve years old and wrote "Gandul's Revenge" when he was eleven. He moved to Ashland, Oregon, before he could do the illustrations, so he let one of his friends do them. He loves to play the trumpet and plays it on the streets of Ashland.

ELLA ASHFORD is twelve years old. She lives half the year in Port Townsend, Washington, and splits the rest of the year between sailing the Hawaiian Islands and snow camping in Manning Provincial Park, Canada. Joining her on these adventures is her mom, dad, two younger brothers, and her teddy bear, Kira, who became real. *Descendants of the Gods* is Ella's first novel. She has an inescapable desire to perpetuate Greek Mythology on her own terms.

ROWAN HALPIN is a fifteen-year-old from a

seaside town in Washington. He lives with his mother and father and younger brother. He enjoys music, playing the drums, and being with friends.

SAM HERON is from Port Townsend, Washington, and has been a writer for five years. At Pato's Cave, Patrick Jennings has mentored Sam into becoming a great writer. By taking these classes, she has built confidence in publishing in little things such as anthologies. She continues to write happily in her home of P.T. She enjoys authors such as Sharon Creech and James Patterson. Her inspirations are Patrick Jennings, James Patterson, and Mia Nebel. She happily attends Blue Heron Middle School as a seventh grader.

ODETTE JENNINGS lives in Port Townsend, Washington, with her parents. She is an only child. She loves to play the piano, write, read, and bike. She has always been fascinated by sharks, especially great whites, and by shark attacks. Mostly she writes realistic fiction. *Red Creek* is her first historical piece. "Miss Delilah" was inspired by Libba Bray's *The Diviners*.

LEMONIE is ten years old and lives in Port Townsend, Washington, with her mom, dad, and brother, Raphael. This is the first story she wrote at Pato's Cave.

E(LIZABETH) M(ARIE) PENROSE lives in Port Townsend, Washington, with three cats, one llama, and one dog. She sometimes has ducks. She hates writing biographies.

KORBYN REIMNITZ has lived in Port Townsend, Washington, his whole life. He began writing his novel when he was twelve and finished it when he was fifteen. It will be the first book in a series of four. It is a fantasy novel featuring magic and mythical creatures, set in a medieval time. It was inspired by other fantasy novels, such as *The Lord of the Rings* and *The Hobbit*. Korbyn hopes to finish all four books during high school and college, and then get them published.

RUEVEAR is a young author, but also an illustrator. She likes writing things that could actually happen, but also things that are just out of this world and very unrealistic. Her parents and brother are all artists. She was taught art by her mother at a very young age. She starts many stories but finishes few. She has finished a short story, is working on a novel, and is in the process of drawing illustrations for her picture book. Ruevear lives in Port Townsend, Washington, with many pets and her family in a round house.

ISAAC STEIMLE is a fourteen-year-old writer of fiction and fantasy. He lives in Port Townsend, Washington, with his parents, older brother, and younger sister. He has two dogs and a cat. His interests include mountain biking, kayaking, and hiking. Some of his favorite books include *The Lord of the Rings*, *The Inheritance Cycle*, and *Ender's Game*. He loves writing and reading all kinds of books.

ANNA TALLARICO was born in Port Townsend, Washington, where she lives with her parents, two black Labrador retrievers, and a cat. She likes anything artistic or sporty, including reading, writing, violin, and dance. *Thunderheart*, published by Arthouse Press, 2013, is her first full-length novel. She finished the first draft when she was ten. She's working on two sequels, and lots of other projects.

STORY WALSH is twelve years old. He lives in Port Townsend, Washington, with his mom, sister, and two dogs. He also lives in Santa Fe, New Mexico, with his dad. In his spare time he likes to read and make things. He prefers to write poems about inanimate objects.

O. J. R. WEINBLATT DEY is a sixth grader

currently living in Port Townsend, Washington. He loves fantasy and adventure stories, which partly inspired him to start writing this novel. He spends a lot of time with his family and enjoys the outdoors. He loves to draw anything that comes to his mind, and is very active.

ELLA WIEGERS is thirteen. She lives with her parents and a book-loving cat. When not writing, Ella likes to dance and to bake French pastries.